Love
There's All Kinds

Ally Allowinter

Acknowledgments

It's the people around us that give us the push we need to write, to print, and to publish. I'm fortunate to have a wonderful family that cheers me on and believes in my writing.

Thank you to the authors who read my work and helped me fix things. Patti, for calling me out on some of my plot issues. Kay, for her excited responses and editing suggestions. Kathy, a voice from across the ocean in Australia, who offered wonderful plot suggestions and a new point of view. Sherri, a romance writer, who offered words of wisdom.

Thank you Karyn Lovern Johnson, for the lovely image and for allowing me to use it on my cover.

To Rachel and Truman, thanks for putting up with all my emails asking what you thought about my writing.

And to Dale, thanks for everything.

Copyright © June, 2025
Publisher: S. McGiboney
ISBN: 978-1-964345-12-3
Library of Congress Control Number: 2025910407

Preface

Can everyone find love?

The answer to that depends upon the definition of the word. For some, it is the all encompassing passion one feels for another human. For others, it may be the gentle companionship of their pet. We all use the word in different ways, but sometimes, it can go wrong.

In a lifetime, one might experience all the ranges of this sometimes elusive feeling. These stories will tug at your heart, make you sad, and might seem impossible.

I hope you enjoy reading them as much as I've enjoyed writing them.

Ally

Contents

The Proposal

Enduring Love

*W*ith each step, Ellie's walker, minus the tennis balls, made rhythmic taps on the tile floor. She stood tall. Her silvery-white hair, gathered into a ponytail below her left ear, fell over her breast like a silken scarf. The dark blue dress contrasted with the light blue of her eyes. On her feet were pink-sequined, but sensible, shoes.

William waited and fidgeted with his tie. When she reached him, he held out his arm to her, like a prince escorting his princess. Ellie let go of the walker and weaved her arm into his.

William's heart sang, pumping with the same childish beat from long ago. Ellie still had dimples. "Hello, Ellie. You look as beautiful as you did when you were ten." Ellie laughed. "And I can see that you haven't lost your charming ways, either."

William was never charming. He was stubborn and tenacious when he was young. At eight years old he was the best newspaper boy in the Kensington neighborhood of Philadelphia.

On a rainy November day in 1935, he carefully placed a newspaper on the porch of a new customer. He didn't want their first paper to be soggy. As he stood to go, the door opened revealing a white angel with flowing long red hair. The words quietly tumbled from his lips. "You are the most beautiful thing I've ever seen. I think I'm going to marry you one day!"

The angelic vision spoke with a rough Irish accent. "Get lost, kid!" The paper disappeared as the door slammed shut.

William learned that Ellie Mae McLaughlin had arrived from New York with her father, who took over managing the local bar and grill. William knew he was in love. It didn't matter that she was two years older. Each day he placed something special alongside the paper, then, after crossing the street and hiding, he watched.

With each flower, Ellie's smile grew. With each poem, her eyes shined brighter. William delighted in her squeal when he left frogs and bugs.

That first Valentine's Day, instead of hiding, he held the paper, knocked, and waited at her door. Ellie opened the door, reaching down to grab the paper. She gave a little shriek when she noticed William standing in front of her.

"What are you doing?"

He wanted to turn and run, but instead, he blurted out the question that he desperately wanted to ask. "Ellie, will you marry me?"

She laughed, grabbed the newspaper out of his hand, and tucked it under her arm. She turned and quietly walked back into the house. She didn't slam the door.

During the following months, he didn't ask her that question again, but he did put on a brave front and asked her if he could buy her things. She nodded.

William spent a large portion of his paper money buying her penny ice-cream sodas and trinkets. They spent time listening to the radio and reading books, aloud, on her porch.

On the next Valentine's Day, he asked again. This time she simply said, "No."

Six years molded William into a handsome, still rosy-cheeked, but strong fourteen-year-old boy. Every day, he and Ellie talked on the porch, but she refused to go places with him, always saying he was too young.

On a cool February day, William asked her if she'd accompany him to the park. She surprised him by agreeing. On the way, he picked wildflowers and presented them to her with a flourish. He sat her down on the bench and asked. "Ellie, will you marry me?"

She smiled, then stood up, walked a few steps down the park trail, and turned. She tilted her head and held out her hand. "Maybe."

William took her hand and they strolled in the park discussing the struggle in Europe. Ellie said she wanted to be a nurse. William told her he wanted to be a pilot.

"No, you can't be a pilot."

"Why not?"

"There's a war starting, you know. All the papers are saying it. You'll get yourself killed."

"Will you miss me?"

Ellie swatted his arm. "You know I would. Please, don't be a pilot."

William felt hopeful as they returned to her house. He patted the pouch in his pocket, confident that she would one day say yes to his marriage proposal. He just knew it!

The following Monday, with high hopes of their future together, William laid the paper on the porch with a red rose. Ellie didn't open the door. Nobody did. William knocked, but there was no answer.

The neighbor saw him and said, "They're gone."

"Gone?"

"Yeah, took a bag each and left town. Didn't you hear? The cops raided the bar last night."

William's heart broke. He fingered the pouch in his pocket. It grew heavy.

In the next few days, the words EMBEZZLEMENT, ILLEGAL, and MOB lined the pages of the newspaper.

William felt his life was over. He pined for three years, never hearing a word from her. He couldn't wait to join the Air Force to fight in the war. With his parents' signature, he joined at age seventeen. Ellie's words rang in his ear, "You'll get yourself killed!" He didn't care. Without her, there was no use living.

But life happened. He survived the last year of the war and a career in the Air Force. He found a new life with a kind woman who died before he retired. When his son and daughter-in-law died in a car crash, he raised his three grandchildren.

Barbara, his youngest grandchild, encouraged him to use Facebook. "Look, Pop-pop, you can keep in touch with me while I am at college. You can see Timmy and Julie, too, back in Philadelphia."

This year, the grandchildren celebrated William's eighty-second birthday during the Christmas break, when everyone could be present.

On the fourth day of January, he sat alone, everyone having returned to their educational pursuits. He opened his Facebook page and smiled at all the silly photos his grandchildren posted from their holiday.

He found himself on Facebook a lot, and usually the digital link to his family kept his melancholy at bay.

But on this day, he was especially lonely. He thought about Ellie. He wondered if she was on the internet, then smacked his head because he hadn't thought of it before.

He slowly typed her name into the search bar but paused before hitting the return key. He held his breath, then pressed the key. He couldn't believe he found her after only three hits on the name "Ellie Mae." There she was! Ellie Mae McLaughlin, now Burke, living across the country in Albuquerque, New Mexico.

He sent a friend request.

The silence was louder than a door slamming. His thoughts screamed, "Maybe she's still married? Maybe she's gone? Maybe she doesn't remember me?"

Like a moth drawn to fire, William looked every day to see if she responded. On the seventh day, William's heart lifted when he saw a response. "William. Is it really you?"

The words wouldn't stop. They had seventy years of stories, hardships, and triumphs to account for. As the weather warmed, so did William's lonely heart.

In May, before he could change his mind, he bought a one-way ticket to Albuquerque. Then he wrote to Ellie, "I'm coming to see you."

Before he left, William dug deep into his old trunk and found the leather pouch. He hadn't opened it since the day he put it away after Ellie disappeared. He pulled out the small silver band, remembering the words his grandmother said when she gave it to him. "I don't need this anymore where I'm going. This will make a nice wedding ring for the girl you fall in love with."

The ring was meant for only one girl.

He packed it with his clothes and booked a flight.

Ellie's retirement home surprised him. It was more like a beautiful, fancy hotel. Very fitting, he thought, for the Ellie that he remembered.

Now here she was, taking his arm. Her blue eyes were as bright as the day he last saw her.

William's heart beat quickly. He inhaled deeply and then quietly said, "I'm too old to get down on one knee, Ellie. But…" He paused, looked into a sea of blue, and then chuckled, "Ah, hell, Ellie. Are you ready to marry me yet?"

Ellie placed her hand on William's wrinkled cheek and smiled. "Yes, William, I will marry you."

If life gives you a second chance

At love or friendship

Take it

No matter how old you are

Beatrice and the Butler

Love Between Friends

*T*hough he could still see his breath in the cold air, Nicolas felt grateful to have a dry place to sleep. He pulled the egg carton under his ear and the threadbare covers up to his shoulders. He didn't know how long it would be before they repaired the iron grate, but for now, the plywood cover kept most of the wind away from him. The vent from the apartment's dryers provided a little warmth, but they didn't run all the time.

The small crack between the plywood and concrete gave him a view of the old building across the street. Every night for the last several nights, an old woman sat in the window and gazed at the streets below. Nicolas curled up under the blanket, envying the woman's warm home.

But then a balding man entered the frame and towered over the old woman. Spittle flew from his mouth as he yelled at her. She covered her face with her hands and he could see her head moving from side to side. After a few moments, the man threw up his hands and walked away from the window.

Nicolas closed his eyes. He felt her pain. It wasn't that long ago when he was sitting in a chair, convulsive sobs raging, as the people he thought were his friends turned on him. The lawyers fought, friends left, and loved ones betrayed him. Nicolas lost everything he cared about.

He thought living in the streets would free him. That people would work together to survive. But every person worried only about themselves. Sometimes, they were as vicious as James, his former friend of thirty-five years. The homeless stole food and blankets like James stole his money and his wife.

Nicolas forgave the homeless. Strangers that fought for their lives in the cold city streets didn't have many choices.

But James and his wife, Tasha, had a choice. They sacrificed him for money.

While he sat in jail, he felt sad for his wife, who, he thought, had been conned as well. As the trial progressed, her betrayal in the courtroom almost killed him.

Tried and sent to prison, Nicolas thought he'd be there forever, but one of the auditors kept digging and found other discrepancies. That caused the detective to keep digging as well.

Nicolas wore orange for eleven months, until the detective found enough evidence to reverse the charges and start a new fraud case against James.

When the prison gate closed behind him, William had nowhere to go. Tasha had encouraged him to put everything in both names. After the cops threw him in jail, she took it all and ran.

Nicolas took to the streets doing what he could to get by. Because he was cleared of all charges, he couldn't use the halfway houses provided by the probation office. He learned the location of all the homeless shelters and food banks, but only used them when the weather was too bad or he felt ill. It was in the shelters, when his possessions disappeared.

The city streets had plenty of places to hide.

The cold seeped in, bringing his mind back to the present. He shivered. Maybe he should risk a night at the shelter. Nicolas glanced up at the window. The old lady was still sobbing. He couldn't help the twinge of jealousy in his voice when he uttered, "What's she still crying for? She's got a roof over her head."

A moment later, the man that had been with her, stormed out of the front door, got into an Audi and drove off.

Concern chased everything else away. He remembered not having any friends to help him. "Ah, shit. What did he do to her?"

Nicolas spent the next five minutes convincing himself that it was none of his business. But she continued to cry in the window.

He gathered the blanket around his shoulders and headed toward the building.

He pressed the button for her unit and the buzzer let him open the door. As he walked up the narrow, dimly lit stairs, he shivered. Where was the warmth that he imagined? He knocked softly on the door that he thought belonged to her.

He heard shuffling and a click, and then the door opened. The woman held a tissue to her eyes, not really looking at him. "Go away, Ivan. I don't need you here."

"I'm not Ivan."

The tissue moved. Her blue eyes noted his dirty coat, faded knit hat, and shoes without laces. "You're the man from the street."

"Yes, sorry. I saw you crying and wanted to make sure you were okay."

She hesitated, then asked him to come in.

"No, I'm not fit to come into your home. Just tell me you're okay and I'll leave."

She brightened like someone turned up a lamp. "Nonsense. It's cold outside. Have some tea at least."

She limped back in and pointed to a wooden chair by an old wooden table. "Sit. I'll bring you a mug."

Nicolas sat. The chair wobbled slightly and he unconsciously rocked back and forth on the back legs. He watched her putter around in the small kitchen. When she returned with two mugs, she looked at him. With one motherly look, Nicolas plopped the chair to the floor, mumbled, "Sorry," and then accepted the offered mug. "Thank you."

"No need to thank me, young man. It is the neighborly thing to do."

She was about to sit but then said, "Oh, dear me, I forgot."

She shuffled back to the kitchen and returned with pie on a plate.

"Now tell me, what is your name?"

"I'm Nicolas, ma'am."

"Nicolas, I'm glad to meet you. My name is Beatrice."

"Nice to meet you, Ms. Beatrice."

"It's just Beatrice. I'm originally from the north, you know."

Nicolas laughed. Their conversation grew from polite inquiries into two hours of shared pleasantries and stories. Beatrice was one of the last tenants in her building. Her son, Ivan, was bullying her to leave.

"My memories are here. I will not leave them."

"Can't they make you leave?"

"No. I own the place, they cannot."

Nicolas knew nothing of tenant law but figured Ivan would find a way soon enough.

"Do you have money? You could go somewhere nice."

"Where would I go? My family says I should move into one of those assisted living places, but we all know those are just expensive waiting rooms. Really, they'd be happy if I just up and died so they can split up my estate."

Nicolas did not doubt her. He knew about the evils of greed.

"Let's not talk about this, shall we? It's nearing Christmas and I cannot get out…" Beatrice pointed at her feet, "Because of my toe."

"I didn't realize, you should have said something. I would have gotten the tea."

"It's almost healed, just a small surgery. I'd like a tree, but Ivan refuses to bring me one."

"Would you like for me to find one for you?"

"Would you?"

"Yes, I've nothing better to do." He glanced at the clock on her wall. "It's only 7. The tree lots will probably still be open."

"Thank you. Yes, please. A big one. One that will reach way up there!" With excitement she swung her arms to the ceiling.

"Would you like anything else while I am out?"

"Could you stop by the bakery and the store? Here, I'll write a list."

When she finished, she handed it to him. Nicolas gathered his blanket and walked toward the door.

"Wait!" Beatrice hobbled to a closet and pulled out a large black coat. "Here, use this. It's cold."

Nicolas thanked her and put on the oversize coat which made him look more like a vagrant than he felt. With her list in hand and a wallet full of cash, Nicolas left on his errands. He marveled that she had just given a stranger, a homeless man, one hundred dollars. She was either very trusting or very desperate.

He went to the tree lot first. There weren't many trees left.

"Hey, you, get away from here. We don't want you hanging around." A man carrying a wooden bat charged out of the little wooden shack behind a sign with tree prices.

"I'm here to buy a tree."

"Yeah, and with what are you going to pay?"

Nicolas lowered his eyes and counted to ten. When he looked up again, he calmly said, "I have money, I will pay."

Nicolas pulled out the fee for the larger tree plus the delivery charge and handed it to the man. He smiled slightly at the salesman's guilty look.

"Sorry, mate," the man said. "We get all kinds coming here to stand under the heat lamps."

Nicolas nodded. "Please, can you have it delivered to this address?"

"I'll do it myself," the man said.

At the store, Nicolas walked up and down the aisles looking for the items on Beatrice's list. He smiled at the security officer, who followed slightly behind him. The officer did not smile back.

After paying, he walked to the bakery expecting it to be closed. In the window, he saw couples sitting at tables drinking, eating, and laughing. So, it was more than just a bakery, he thought. A twinkly bell chimed when he opened the door. "Happy holidays!" came a soft voice from the back. "I'll be right there!"

The couples turned their heads away from him. The woman came around the corner and froze. "I don't keep much cash in the till!"

Nicolas calmly asked, "May I have two loaves of rye bread?" He looked at the list, "A dozen scones and two slices of chocolate cake?"

The woman blushed and swiftly filled the order. Once it was put in a large bag, she placed it on the counter and stepped back. "Here you go, that will be twenty-four dollars."

He saw the relief in her eyes when he pulled out his wallet. He threw three tens on the counter and gently took the bag. "Keep the change."

The tree arrived just after he did. Beatrice had cleared a corner by the window. Boxes of all sizes were piled on the couch.

"Please put the tree in front of the window," she directed.

The tree man did as he was asked but turned and said, "Do you have a stand? I can help you get it up."

Beatrice beamed, rifled through the largest box, and pulled out the stand.

Nicolas helped the man set up the tree. As the man left, Beatrice handed him something. "Merry Christmas!" she said.

The man tipped an imaginary hat and returned the greeting before leaving.

Gleaming, Beatrice clapped her hands. "Now, let's decorate!"

They pulled ornaments out of the boxes. Beatrice headed for the tree with two ornaments in her hands but Nicolas stopped her. "Do you have lights? They should go on first."

"Oh yes, I think they are in that box over there."

After they hung the last ornament, Beatrice sat back on the couch, the reflection of the tree's white lights glistening on her gray hair. She looked happy.

As he tidied the empty boxes, Nicolas noticed her eyes drooping.

"Beatrice, it has been a wonderful evening. Thank you so much for the food and the merriment. I must go now."

"You can't go out there!" Beatrice protested. "It's too cold. I have a perfectly good bed in my spare room. You shall sleep there."

"No, I can sleep in my home across the street."

Beatrice saw the pride in Nicolas and changed tactics.

"Well, if you won't sleep here, then at least take the pile of blankets from the closet. I don't need them anymore and perhaps you can find a use for them."

"Yes, ma'am."

Nicolas, laden with thick blankets, bid goodnight to Beatrice. The tiny concrete house had never felt so warm.

In the morning, he heard a bird chirping his name. No, wait. Birds wouldn't be calling his name. He opened his eyes. Beatrice, dressed in her nightgown, was holding open the door to the complex, calling his name.

"Nicolas, wake up. I need your help!"

Nicolas threw off the blankets, the cold biting his exposed limbs, and ran to her.

"What, what do you need? Are you hurt?" Nicolas shifted from foot to foot, trying to get the feeling back into his toes.

"No, nothing like that, Nicolas. I need you to deliver this for me, pronto." She held a thick envelope with the address of a local law office on it.

"Can you not use the post?"

"No, it will not be quick enough." She looked in the envelope, folded back the top, and thrust the envelope into his hands. "Hurry. It is Christmas Eve and they will not stay open long. When you deliver it, please stay and wait for them to answer. I need to get the answer."

"Okay, if it is that important to you, I will."

The ten-minute walk warmed him. He pulled the envelope from the deep pockets of his new coat, and stared at the door, unsure if he should walk right in or knock. He knocked.

A young woman, her brown hair pulled into a bun and wearing a neatly tailored suit, answered the door. A string of blinking Christmas lights adorned her neck.

"Come in, quickly, before all the hot air gets out."

"No, thank you. I just came to deliver this. I will wait outside until you respond."

"We have hot chocolate and cake?"

Nicolas took only seconds to change his mind. "Okay, thank you." He followed her inside.

The woman walked to a table piled with colorful plates and all kinds of food. She placed a few things on a plate, grabbed a mug of steaming liquid, and brought it back to him. "Here you go. You can sit there," she pointed at the leather chairs near a crackling fire, "until I return."

Nicolas admired that she didn't flinch at his appearance, but he did not sit.

When she returned, she handed him back the envelope. It was thinner now. "Please return this to Mrs. Polanski."

"Is that Beatrice?"

"Yes." The woman smiled and then looked at the empty plate in Nicolas's other hand. "I'll take care of that for you. Run along."

Nicolas felt like a child being told what to do, but he did it anyway.

He knocked lightly on Beatrice's door. He recognized the shuffling sound before Beatrice opened the door. She had changed into day clothes. Her worried frown turned upside down. "Oh, Nicolas, you are back. I am so glad you are back."

"Why wouldn't I come back? And, in the future, don't ever prop that front door open again. I could have been a robber or something."

"Why wouldn't you indeed? And reprimand noted. Please, come sit a spell."

Beatrice had set out the bread from last night along with meats, cheeses, fruit, and jellies.

"So where will you go for Christmas?" Nicolas asked.

"Nowhere, I am staying right here."

"Aren't you going to go with family?"

"No. They are heading to the Bahamas or some such place. Why would I want to drag my old bones there? Truly, they should, or at least one of them, stay with me, but they are beggars and think only of themselves."

Beatrice gave Nicolas a pointed look. "You have been more like family to me in two days than any of my progeny have been over the last five years."

Nicolas decided to do something about the sadness he heard. "Do you play cards, Beatrice?"

"Yes, I love to play Rummy."

"Do you have any cards?"

Beatrice pulled cards from a drawer, pulled off the rubber band, and placed them on the table. She then rummaged through a few desk drawers and returned to the table with a paper and pencil.

"I'll keep score. My late husband was known to flip numbers around and I don't trust anyone else to do it."

"Fine by me! Shall I cut the cards?"

They played until Beatrice heard a growl from Nicolas's stomach. They ordered Chinese food to be delivered. While they waited, Beatrice offered for Nicolas to pick out some of her late husband's clothes and take a shower.

"I can shower at the YMCA."

"But it won't open until the day after Christmas. You are here, there are plenty of towels and lots of clothes to choose from. Why not?"

Nicolas couldn't think of a reason except pride. But he wanted to make her happy. He chose a pair of slacks, a shirt, and some underclothes from a drawer. The shower felt great. He found an old razor under the sink and used it to remove his scraggly beard.

Beatrice laughed when he returned.

"What, do I have a cut on my face or something?"

"No, Nicolas. You look wonderful…if a little too tall for George's slacks."

Nicolas smiled. The pants were two inches too short and the wide waist band crinkled under the belt he used to hold them up. He looked ridiculous but felt clean.

"You can take your clothes and throw them in the washer. Your coat too. I have a very large washer."

Nicolas did as he was told.

The food arrived. Beatrice picked at hers but enjoyed eating it. "I haven't had Chinese food in a while. That was so good."

"It was good, thank you."

Beatrice sat up straighter, her eyes narrowed slightly and her mouth set in a grim line. "Nicolas, have you no place to go? Nobody to be with?"

"No, ma'am. I do not."

"Would you consider being my butler?"

Nicolas almost spit out the sip of tea he had just taken. "Your what?"

"My butler. I need help in this apartment and you need a place to live. I think it would be a great arrangement. I'll pay you."

"Beatrice, I can accept your offer of a job on one condition."

"What is that?"

"You allow me to sleep in my own home."

Beatrice pursed her lips and glanced out the window at the wooden door to Nicolas's cave. Then she relaxed and said, "Fine. But you will take showers and do all your laundry here."

"Okay."

"Good. Now…" Beatrice stood up. "Just two things. From now on you can call me Tess." She stood up, reached into her purse and pulled out a set of keys. "Do you know how to drive?"

"Yes, but…"

"That's all that matters. We are going out."

After he helped her with her coat and down the two flights of stairs, Beatrice handed him the keys. "The car is parked in the building in the back. You'll see some garage doors; ours is number 2A. Please pull it around."

Nicolas walked around to the back and saw the row of garage doors. Most were half open. Door 2A had a shiny lock on it. He fiddled with different keys until he found one that opened it. The heavy door moved sluggishly as he lifted it. Then he saw what was inside.

"Would you look at that!" Nicolas whistled. He opened the door and slid behind the wheel of the 1975 Chevy Caprice Classic. He inserted the key and turned his wrist. It took a few moments of sputtering tires, then the engine came to life.

The week of Christmas flew by. Each day was something different. Now that Beatrice had a willing driver and friend, she wanted to go everywhere. She insisted that Nicolas buy pants that fit. He insisted it would come out of his first paycheck.

But as the New Year approached, Nicolas noticed that Beatrice wasn't moving around so well. "It's okay. I'm just not used to all this adventure." She beamed.

On January 3, Nicolas drove Beatrice to the same lawyer's office. "Please wait in the car, I won't be long."

She came out huffing. "Why must they insist on this nonsense?" She looked at Nicolas and handed him a business card. "Please, can you take me to this address."

Beatrice stormed into the therapist's office. "I need to see Dr. Hamilton."

A middle-aged woman looked annoyed. "He's not free at the moment. Do you have an appointment?"

"Just tell him Mrs. Polanski is here to see him. It will only take a moment."

The woman picked up the phone, said a few words, and hung up. "He'll be right out. Please take a seat."

"I don't need to take a seat."

The door to the inner office opened and Dr. Hamilton greeted Beatrice with a hug. "Tess, what brings you by today?"

Beatrice thrust a piece of paper into Dr. Hamilton's hands. "Please fill this out so I can take care of my business."

Dr. Hamilton skimmed over the paper and laughed. "Really, they need this? Okay."

He took a pen off the desk and filled out the form, then glanced at his secretary. "Can you put your fingers on my notary stamp?"

The secretary harrumphed but dutifully pulled out the device. After Dr. Hamilton made the mark, he folded the paper, stuffed it into an envelope with his logo on it, sealed it, then handed it back to Beatrice.

"There you go, Tess. Why they needed me to sign off on your sanity is beyond me. You are the most put-together lady I have ever met."

"I knew I could count on you, Dr. Hamilton."

"Any time!"

Beatrice returned to the car and directed Nicolas to return to the lawyer's office. "I want you to come in with me this time."

"It's not necessary. I can wait here."

"No, I want your support."

"If you insist."

They walked into the building and were immediately directed into an office. Beatrice handed the envelope from Dr. Hamilton to Mr. Parker. Then she introduced Nicolas to Mr. Parker and his partner, Mr. Burle. "This is Nicolas. He is my butler and driver. He is the gentleman I have been discussing with you earlier. Will there be any more difficulties with my request?"

"No, ma'am," they responded in unison.

"Thank you."

With that, Beatrice turned and sauntered out of the room. "Come along, Nicolas."

Nicolas held the door for her to get into the car. After she sat, she grabbed her chest and her breathing became erratic.

Nicolas immediately knelt, taking her hand into his. "Tess, are you all right?"

It took a moment, but Beatrice nodded, then quietly asked to be taken home. She slept the remainder of the day.

In the three weeks that followed, Nicolas and Beatrice formed a routine. He would arrive at her door at 8, take a shower, and change. They'd enjoy a light breakfast and then he'd drive her around the city. Some days it was a trip to the park. Other days it would be a trip to the department store where Beatrice would buy children's clothing and toys.

"Why are you buying all that? Do you have grand-kids?"

"None that don't come with strings attached. I buy all this for the orphanage and the hospital. And you, my good friend, will be my Santa."

Most days, they ate lunch at the nearest cafe or restaurant, then returned to Beatrice's to play a game of cards or a board game. They often ate takeout for dinner but sometimes Nicolas would cook.

On a cold morning, Nicolas arrived for breakfast but while they ate, the electricity went out.

"That's strange?" Beatrice put down her napkin and walked over to the credenza and found a recent bill. She called the number. After a series of artificial voices, a person finally answered. "New York, electric, please state your name, account number, and problem."

Beatrice glanced at the bill and read all the information and ended with, "Is there a problem with the electricity on my block? Mine is no longer working."

"Just a moment." After what felt like five minutes, the man returned. "Ma'am, there aren't any power outages in your area. But we do have an order in the system from your account that says the place is abandoned and to shut it off."

"Well, sir, it is certainly not abandoned. I still live here and I need my electricity."

Nicolas, overhearing most of the conversation through Beatrice's cell phone, gently pried the phone out of her shaking hands. "Sir, please turn back on the electricity. Is there a date on that order?"

"I can't say, sir?"

"Look, I don't want to have to call my lawyer, but it seems that her account was hacked and I want to know who did it?

The poor guy seemed flustered. "Fine, fine, no need for lawyers. Wait a minute."

Nicolas heard the tapping of the keyboard, then the man came back on. "Looks like an Ivan Polanski wrote us a few weeks ago and set this date. There's an attached power of attorney, otherwise we wouldn't have done it since the account is in Beatrice Polanski's name."

Nicolas hit mute and asked Beatrice, "Did you give Ivan a power of attorney?"

She shook her head. "Never."

Turning the sound back on, Nicolas politely asked, "Could you send me a copy of that? I believe it's a fake."

"I will, but don't go telling anyone who sent it to you."

"Don't worry, you are not the issue here."

Nicolas provided the man his personal email address, the one he kept active but only looked at in the library since he didn't have a laptop, then ended the call. He handed the phone back to Beatrice. "Looks like Ivan is playing tricks on you."

Beatrice swore, then called Ivan. "Look, Ivan, I don't know how you managed to turn off my electricity, but I am not leaving, even if I have to buy propane heaters. Do you understand that?" She ended the call without waiting for a response.

A few days later, while Nicolas cooked dinner, the front door buzzed. Beatrice walked over to the speaker and pressed the button.

"Hey, you should really ask who's there before letting them in."

She laughed. "It's not like there is anyone else they want to see here. It's fine, it's probably a…" She was interrupted by the knock on her door.

She partially opened it and stared at a middle-aged man wearing a suit and holding a clipboard. A police officer stood slightly behind him.

"Mrs. Polanski?"

"Yes?"

"My name is Robert Barnes and I'm from the department of health.

Officer Romani and I are here to do a wellness check."

"Why on earth would you need to do that."

"We have a complaint here stating that you are over the age of eighty, living alone, that you have difficulty walking, and that your housing area presents a danger to your welfare. It's just routine, ma'am."

"Well, I never!" Beatrice huffed, her breathing becoming ragged. Nicolas walked up behind her and put his hand on her shoulder. His warmth calmed her down.

"Ma'am, may we come in?"

Beatrice pulled the door open all the way. "Enter and see that I'm absolutely fine. I am not alone. I have my butler to take care of me. Obviously, I can walk just fine since I answered the door, and if you dare to believe your senses, we were just about to eat a healthy bowl of chicken soup."

Robert had the grace to look embarrassed before he entered her apartment, followed by Officer Romani. "It sure does smell good."

Smiling, Beatrice asked, "Would you care to join us?"

Robert looked at Officer Romani and shrugged, "You were our last inspection for today. Sure, if you have enough."

Nicolas finally spoke. "We have plenty, I'll get you both a bowl. Please have a seat."

After an hour of good food and conversation, Robert stood. "Thank you, Beatrice and Nicolas, for a wonderful meal." He grabbed his clip board and wrote something on it, then handed it to Beatrice.

She read it aloud so Nicolas could hear. "The complaint is untrue. Beatrice Polanski is thriving in a clean environment and cared for by her wonderful companion. No action is needed. End report."

Beatrice watched them from the window as they got into Officer Romani's vehicle. "I'll bet I know who made that complaint." She pulled the curtains closed and sighed as she sat in a chair. "Will they ever stop badgering me?"

Not knowing how to answer that, Nicolas stayed silent.

The following Sunday, Beatrice announced that she wanted to go to church. Nicolas pulled into the parking lot and helped her out of the car.

She took his hand and stared into his eyes. "Will you come in with me?"

Nicolas did not want to go to church. He lowered his head so that Beatrice couldn't see his feelings on the matter. "I'll go to the cafe and come back when it's over."

She didn't argue but as she walked toward the church, she wobbled slightly. He cursed his pride.

Slamming the car door, he caught up to her and took her arm. "Let me help you."

He didn't see the slight smile on Beatrice's face as he escorted her to a pew in the back. When she sat, she tugged on his arm. Her woeful expression made Nicolas feel like a ten-year-old again. "Please sit?"

Nicolas sat.

After the service, Beatrice decided they should eat lunch in style. "I want to eat at the Steak House on Broad, will you dine with me, please, Nicolas?"

"But I thought you don't eat steak because of your teeth or something."

"No, I don't eat the steak, but they have other wonderful food and I love their cheesecake. Please say you'll come to eat with me?"

"I'm not dressed properly."

"That's easily remedied." Beatrice certainly had a way of getting Nicolas to do what she wanted. The word "no" disappeared when she asked for things.

She waited in the car while Nicolas changed into "the right clothes," which included an old sport coat of her late husband's.

He held his breath while he drove, not sure he'd be able to enter the place. He'd never eaten there, but wanted to take his wife on their anniversary. The memory of her deceit stung him again.

Beatrice made a delighted sound when they pulled up to the valet parking. "It's been years since I've eaten here."

Her infectious happiness overcame all his bad memories.

The restaurant lived up to its reputation, and the cheesecake made him even happier.

Afterward, the valet pulled up with their car, got out, and opened the door for Beatrice. Nicolas helped Beatrice get into the passenger seat. Before he could shut the door, he watched her grab her chest.

"Tess, what's wrong?"

She couldn't answer for a moment, then took a deep breath. She tried to speak but it was soft and weak. "I'm okay, let's go home."

She wasn't okay. Her face paled and her breath came in spurts. "You need to see a doctor. I'm taking you to the ER."

Nicolas ran around to the driver's seat, started the car, and quickly drove to the hospital that was five blocks away.

After calling the lawyer's office and asking them to call her family, he waited in the lobby. Several strangers sat, then left. More came and went. Finally, a doctor nodded toward him.

"Are you Nicolas?"

"Yes, how is she?"

"She's stable, but very fragile."

"Can I see her?"

"Not tonight. She said you should go home, to her home."

"I'm sure she did."

"If you don't have more questions, I need to move on."

"No. Thank you, doctor."

Nicolas got another cup of coffee and sat down again.

"Nicolas? Are you Nicolas?"

Nicolas came out of the darkness of a deep sleep with a grunt and shake of his head. "What?"

"Are you Nicolas?" the tiny woman in a nurse's uniform asked again.

"Yes."

"Follow me, please."

Nicolas followed her to the ICU and through a set of double doors. They handed him a mask and gown and then directed him through a door.

Beatrice was lying quietly with an IV in her arm. At her request, they had removed all the other monitors. He noted a flower arrangement on a table nearby and glanced at the card. The lawyer's office that he called had sent a bouquet of roses.

She smiled. "Nicolas, my friend. I knew you'd still be here."

"Tess, you old coot, you scared me."

"No need to be scared."

"Have any of your family been in touch?"

She frowned. "I don't want to talk about them." Beatrice started coughing and Nicolas ran to hand her a tissue. "Listen, I have to ask you for one more favor."

"Anything."

"Don't say no!"

"What?"

"Just don't say no. Accept the gift as it's given."

"But…"

Beatrice coughed again. This time, Nicolas hurried to get her a glass of water.

"Please," she asked again.

"Fine."

"Fine what?" she slyly repeated.

"Fine, I will not say no. I will accept the gift."

"Good."

Nicolas took Beatrice's hand in his. She patted their hands with her other hand and repeated, "Good."

She closed her eyes, then opened them and asked, "Nicolas?"

"Yes, Tess?"

"Will you please sleep in the apartment tonight?"

"Yes."

"And every other night? I don't want to worry about you being on the streets."

"Yes, I will. Don't you worry about me."

"No, now I won't."

The nurse returned and shooed Nicolas away. He kissed Beatrice lightly on the forehead. She didn't open her eyes but she smiled.

Beatrice stayed in the hospital for two more nights. On the third day, holding Nicolas's hand, she died. Before she closed her eyes for the final time, she reminded Nicolas, "Remember, you promised."

"I remember."

None of her family called or visited her in the hospital.

Besides Nicolas, only Ivan and another woman, who Nicolas guessed was his wife, came to her funeral.

All four of her children attended the lawyer's office on the day of the will reading.

Nicolas felt out of place in the lawyer's office. The four siblings dressed to match the size of their trust funds. He could smell greed in the room and saw the smiles grow on their faces as the lawyer outlined the massive estate which included the apartment complex and the block of land it sat upon, the contents of her apartment, the car, all of her savings, and a large investment portfolio.

After a pause, Mr. Burle cleared his throat. He then read aloud the health report from Mr. Barnes and the declaration of sanity from Dr. Hamilton.

"Would anyone like to go over these documents?"

Nobody spoke.

Mr. Burle cleared his throat and asked, "Does anyone here question Beatrice Pulaski's state of mind upon hearing this testimony?"

"No. Just get on with it." Nicolas recognized Ivan, the balding man who made Beatrice cry.

"Then I shall." The lawyer turned the page of the document. He took a moment to lock eyes with each individual who was present.

He inhaled then exhaled. "Remember, this is legally binding and cannot be changed."

He then read the last paragraph of Beatrice's last will and testament.

"All family and friends attending me upon my death shall inherit equal portions of my heretofore mentioned estate."

Renovating for Revenge

Broken Love

Also published in

Bonfire: A Campfire Anthology

by the Pamlico Writers Group

September 22, 2022 ISBN:979-8352100912

Daryl's smile grew as Wyatt Earp's bushy brown eyebrows oozed over the wax figure's finely crafted nose. He aimed the blow torch lower. Even better was the way the eyes drooped, weeping black, blue, and white streaks, like war paint, over Wyatt's tanned, waxy cheeks.

He stepped back to view his work, wiping his sweaty hands through his short blond hair. The lifelike wax figure stood in a recreated saloon. The faded bar was behind it and its right hand rested on the wood. The figure's left hand rested on the hilt of a fake gun in a holster.

Daryl started melting Wyatt first because of how much the statue looked like his boss, Barry.

After a few minutes of intense heat, Wyatt's face looked more like Sasquatch's. Long, sad, and ugly. He wished he could make Barry's real face look that way. But Daryl's lanky frame was no match for Barry's football physique. The wax figure was going to have to do.

The melted face mirrored how Daryl felt. "Take that, you dirty, cheating SOB!"

Daryl did odd construction jobs for a living. It allowed him to explore the country. His high school friend Barry had asked him to come to Tombstone and do a job for him. He hadn't been out west, so he figured, "Why not?"

The job was to renovate the back half of Barry's building. "Can you do it at night when the place is closed so the noise doesn't bother the visitors?"

He'd been working at it for about five months and didn't have a problem working at night, until now. He was halfway into putting up the framing for the extra closet when his drill gave out. His spare battery was still at the trailer a few miles up the road. Moving in with his new girlfriend, Star, four months ago, saved him a lot of money. He cut off the power, locked the building, and headed home to get what he needed.

As he pulled in front of the trailer, he noticed Barry's truck in the grassy driveway. "That's odd!"

He walked up the wooden stairs to the front door. That's when he heard the noise. He quietly opened the door. He didn't want to scare them if they were watching a movie. But it wasn't a movie they were watching. There was no mistaking the long, shapely legs that were wrapped around a naked Barry or the moans that Star uttered during sex.

He'd forgiven her once for "accidentally" kissing a guy when she was drunk. The second time she did something stupid he almost believed her story. "I was drunk, and he took advantage." But this? There's no way this wasn't planned. Daryl wondered how long Barry had been banging Star while smiling at him every night when he came to work.

Darryl backed out of the door quietly and tiptoed to his truck. He reversed out of the driveway, then drove to a shadowy part of the gas station across the street and parked. He opened his phone. Star answered on the third ring. He blurted out, "Hey, honey, I think I'm gonna be here a little longer tonight. I want to get this frame finished so I can start the drywall tomorrow. Probably won't be back until after midnight. You okay with that?"

"Oh, hi, Barry," she said breathlessly. "Sure, whatever."

"Are you okay? You sound a little winded?"

Star coughed, "Yeah, I'm okay. I was just taking out the trash."

"Okay, then. I'll try not to wake you when I get home."

Barry ended the call. He knew Star. Knowing he would be late would be all she needed to venture out to do what she always did. Play pool and get drunk at the Tombstone Saloon. Even better, she'd drag big ol' Barry with her to buy all her drinks.

He wanted to hurt Barry, but that would be suicide. Barry had at least 150 pounds on him. He was done with Star too. He wasn't sure he ever really loved her, but the idea of being settled had appeal.

His thoughts were interrupted as he watched Star and Barry get into Barry's truck and leave the trailer. When they were out of view, Daryl drove back to the trailer, loaded up the belongings he cared about, and then headed back to the museum. He still had tools to collect.

The idea struck when he walked into the building and saw all Barry's beloved statues.

"So," Daryl thought, "you want to refurbish the place? Well, I'll do that, all right!"

But after spending so much time on Wyatt, Daryl was miffed that the wax didn't drip quickly enough like those cheap candles placed in wine bottles tended to do. At this rate, he wouldn't get many of the statues refurbished Daryl style. He might as well go with demolition.

He picked up the machete from the wax explorer scene. He tested the blade. "Ow, shit, it's sharp." He was about to take a whack at Wyatt when the wax figure's head rolled off.

That gave him another idea.

He walked over to the statue of Pocahontas. He always wondered what the hell Pocahontas was doing in the Wild West. Using the machete, he swiped at her neck. Her head rolled into the fake Chickahominy River. He picked up her head and brought it over to Wyatt's headless form. He reached out to see if the wax on Wyatt's neck was still hot.

"Ouch, shit!"

Yep, still hot. He then placed Pocahontas's head on top of the cowboy's body.

Stepping back he admired his alien-like creation.

"Now this is progress."

He inventoried the rest of the occupants of "Big Barry's Wax Emporium."

"Well, I declare," Daryl said out loud to nobody. "I never thought I could rewrite the past."

Four hours later, after a few burned fingertips and a small cut on the palm of his hand, history at Barry's had a whole new twist. Columbus was now married to Mrs. Nixon. Mrs. Bush was a Cro-Magnon's wife, and there were several human bodies with animal heads and wild animals sporting heads from the U.S. Calvary men.

To make sure his message was understood, Daryl lifted Wyatt's body with Pocahontas's head onto the bar. He ripped open the shirt and undid the belt buckle, letting the gun belt hang askew. He then placed Calamity Jane, with her leggings pulled down to her ankles, on top in such a manner that one would not doubt that the two wax figures were having passionate sex. Only now, Calamity had a rattlesnake for a head.

Daryl was pleased with the results. He laughed. It came out slowly at first, just a low rumble in the back of his throat. Soon he was laughing so hard tears were running down his eyes.

He wiped away the tears and a fleeting thought of sadness came over him. "Damn, I wish I could be here to see Barry's face!"

Surveying the scene one last time, Daryl knew he'd punched Barry where it hurt the most. "Serves you right! Asshole!" he muttered.

Daryl carefully placed the machete back into the hands of the African tour guide. He didn't want the guide's new Marilyn Monroe head to fall off.

He made sure the torch was cleaned off and placed back in the workroom.

After he collected his tools and placed them in the cab of his truck next to his suitcase and favorite pillow, he turned and slowly walked back into the museum. There was a bit of burnt smell in the air. He didn't care. He set the alarm and carefully closed the door, locking it behind him.

There weren't any cameras in this part of Tombstone. The "Old West" mock town was always a ghost town at night. Daryl put the key under the mat where Barry would find it on Monday morning.

He climbed into his truck, started the engine, and sat for a few minutes. He'd already been south. He was from the East and didn't want to go back yet. The West hadn't been too kind to him. North. That's where he'd go. He drove away with no particular destination in mind whistling a tune he'd heard on the radio. "He had it coming!"

Revenge

The desire to act upon those who wronged us can be strong

Whatever you do, don't hurt the physical person

Just screw up their life

Otherwise it's just murder

The Mother-In-Law

Love Beyond Morals

I hoisted her over the bridge's railing, her arms flopping around like a rag doll. I wouldn't have thought of this problem-solving idea if I hadn't remembered my second-grade tormentor. He was a foul-mouthed neighbor boy who delighted in telling me gory details about how he killed things. The deer stories I could handle, lots of people went hunting, but the kittens got to me. You see, they had a lot of cats that weren't spayed. Rather than take care of that detail, they just got rid of the kittens when they came. He and his brothers would stuff the kittens in a bag and throw them over the bridge. They'd cheer when the bag splashed in the water and floated for a while, the muffled yet desperate cries of the kittens barely audible over the roaring of the river. They took bets on how long it would take before the silence came.

When she landed, the splash wasn't as loud as I thought it would be. She didn't thrash around. The sedatives running through her veins silenced her voice.

She kind of floated for a moment, her mouth opening and closing like a goldfish in a bowl. When the water rose above her nose, her eyes grew large, as if pleading for help.

For a second, I felt something creep into my head. "What did I just do?"

But I shook that thought out of my head. "You shouldn't have tried to take him away from me." I watched until, eventually, she disappeared.

I checked the area to make sure I hadn't dropped anything on the bridge, closed the passenger door, and then walked to the driver's side. When I sat behind the wheel, I glanced in the mirror. I didn't look any different. My brown eyes and brown hair didn't give anything away. Guilt and remorse entered my brain. With shaking hands, I pulled a photo out of my purse and stared at it, breathing deeply until I calmed down. When my hands were stable, I started the engine and spoke out loud. "Problem solved."

Five days later I scanned a newspaper article about the discovery of her body. "Woman found drowned in Pegan River." I read on to see that the police were ascribing it to an accidental suicide. "Poor woman, she was under so much stress!" one quote said. Another person said, "She was always an emotional woman."

I scoffed. Demonic, paranoid, and overbearing were the words I would have used to describe her.

I didn't meet her until after I married Derrick. Ours was a whirlwind romance and elopement. I was in love. I did everything to make him happy and soon discovered that making him "happy" meant making his mother happy too.

He introduced me to her at a Christmas party. I wanted to kill Derrick because his family's idea of casual didn't match mine. Even in my designer jeans and cashmere sweater, I felt unfashionable compared to the other guests. While we waited in line to speak to his mother, like at a funeral reception, I fought to keep embarrassment at bay.

Derrick introduced me like a piper announcing the prince. "Mother, this is Sarah." He waved his arms toward me.

Mother's syrupy voice, and the southern accent that went with it, intensified. She took my hand. "It's so nice to meet you…" She paused, tapped my hand like she was soothing a baby, then turned to her son and asked, "What did you call her?"

"Mother, I told you already, her name is Sarah."

"Ah, yes, Sally. Please, call me Margaret. After all, we are going to be family, aren't we?" I thought that odd since everyone else called her Maggie.

The woman, known to all as Mrs. Margaret Grace Chapman, had some sway in this town, but it wasn't all because of her money. No. Something else, an intangible field, like an invisible string, directed those around her. She'd nod her head and a person would stop talking. She pointed, and someone knew to get her another drink. I watched as the simple act of closing her eyes made a speaker change their opinion.

"I thought the mayor's speech had some merit to it."

BLINK

"But only the part where he said hello."

"I like the Pirates."

BLINK

"But they play awful."

The longer you knew her, the faster you needed to react. The shorter your string, the more power she had over you. Was it Voodoo? Is there Voodoo in the sleepy town of Wayside, Virginia?

In our first three years of marriage, Margaret's interference tested my patience, but I played along. After all, she was my mother-in-law and I wanted Derrick to be happy. But I hadn't realized that I had a string, or how short it had become, until she tugged too hard.

When Margaret invited us to a fancy shindig at her house, I knew something was up. Derrick's profits from his new venture were almost enough to pay back the loan she gave us. But I never knew, until that night, what kind of interest she charged or what demands she would excavate from Derrick's soul.

I sipped my Cabernet and tried to be invisible. When she sashayed directly toward me, I knew something was up.

"Darling," she said in that syrupy, southern voice, "do you see that woman over there?"

Of course I saw the woman. Who could miss the big-boobed brunette who originated in our small town but was now a lead reporter for the big-city newspaper? Taking a sip of her rum and Coke, she continued. "Derrick needs her support, so anything you can do to help him with this relationship would be wonderful. They'll be spending a lot of time together getting his campaign off the ground."

I almost choked on my wine. "Campaign?"

"Didn't Derrick tell you, dear?" From the astonished look on my face, I knew that she knew I had no idea what she was rattling on about. Her gleeful smile was accompanied by the proclamation, "Derrick's going to run for mayor."

Being the mayor of Wayside wasn't much to brag about, but it didn't take a huge brain to figure out that Margaret aspired for her baby boy to end up in Washington.

I rolled my eyes as if it was old news. "Oh, why yes, he did mention it to me," I lied. "But he said he wasn't sure about it at the time."

Margaret's smile did not reach her eyes, but it showed the extensive workmanship of her dentist. "Why then, you'll understand, dear, the sacrifices one has to make?"

Shortly after that night, I discovered I was pregnant. We hoped and prayed this one would last. Two others ended in miscarriage followed by a mandatory parade of doctors, directed by Margret, of course, to ensure my body was all right. This time, I didn't tell anyone until the danger of a miscarriage passed.

"Well, it's about time," she said. "Darling, go get a bottle of wine and we'll celebrate." She looked down at me. "But not for you, dear. You'll have to do better now about keeping up your nutrition."

She took the glass from Derrick and raised it in the air. "Here's to a new chapter in Chapman history." After a sip, she asked, "Derrick, have you told your campaign manager yet? This will be wonderful for your image. Now they'll see you as a family man as well as a smart candidate."

"Family man," I thought. "Funny, wasn't he already a family man with me as his wife?"

Margaret would never knit a blanket, or change a diaper, but she mapped out my unborn child's future before I even got to see his face.

The Derrick I met four years ago, the caring man who put me before anything, disappeared. I wondered how he had escaped the puppet master's clutches to go to a small college three towns away? I supposed her husband was alive then. I tried cajoling, bickering, and bribing, but Margaret controlled my husband.

After Brendan's birth, I had no energy to battle over Derrick's attentions. I let her have him. Brendan brought so much joy to me, even with his colicky cries and spit-up.

Margaret hired a nanny. We didn't need one. I certainly didn't go anywhere. I blamed the fatigue for not fighting that one. I played the dutiful wife with the dutiful house, and let the dutiful nanny visit. Until one day, when I came back early from a doctor's appointment with Brendan and caught the nanny taking pictures of a naked man in our bedroom. After that, I refused to hire another nanny. I felt energized. I won a battle.

Derrick loved his son like a boy loved a puppy. "Good boy, you're walking." Tap, tap, tap on the head. Hugs weren't allowed when Derrick wore a suit, which was most of the time. Snuggles only happened in Brendan's room with Mommy.

"Honey," I pleaded. "Why won't you let him sleep in our bed."

"He might urinate in it. I will not sleep in a bed that has been soiled."

Derrick, it seemed, did not know how to love a child.

We muddled through. I didn't think anyone's marriage was perfect, and we found a rhythm that, while not quite as loving as our courtship, kept us together. At times I thought another woman might have entered his life, but I could not find any proof of it.

Brendan was four and in preschool, one carefully vetted by the mother-in-law, when I returned to my freelance graphic design business. Mostly, I worked from home but sometimes I needed to see a client's building to get ideas or take fresh images for the layouts.

Though I preferred sunsets, the early-morning light covered the mountains behind the hotel in a welcome light. As I photographed the panoramic view, I saw a man walk out the front door. On his arm, a shapely woman beamed at him. I was far enough away that I couldn't make out who they were, but the body language told the story of what they were.

I felt lucky. I wouldn't need to get a model release and if I recognized them later, I could blur them a bit more.

The man crossed the parking lot and got into a red Audi. I shook my head. Derrick and his red Audi were at a conference eight hours away. He should be home tonight.

Imagine my surprise when I pulled into the house and there was his car. I walked into the study where he was pouring himself a whiskey. "What are you doing home so early?"

He caught the glass before it fell, but whiskey hit the counter before he turned to me.

"Sarah." He looked me up and down. I had dressed casually but professionally, a look I used to use all the time. "You look great. Where's Brendan?"

"He's in school."

Derrick knocked back his drink and wiped his mouth with the back of his hand. "Let me get this trip grime off of me and I'll tell you about it."

Without waiting for my answer, he swept by me. About fifteen minutes later, freshly showered and shaved, he came up behind me while I waited for my pictures to upload on my computer. He smelled of memories and nuzzled the back of my neck. "Sarah, I've missed you."

Starving for attention, I ignored the nagging voice in my head asking me, "What's he up to?"

We made love, just like we used to in college. Afterward, he fell into a deep sleep but my brain buzzed. I picked up our clothes which were strewn all over the floor and went to dump them in the basket. That's when I noticed his work shirt with lipstick on it. It wasn't mine. I stopped wearing lipstick because it got all over Brendan when we played together.

A thought bounced into my brain. I plowed through images on my laptop until I found them. I zoomed in and almost threw up. There weren't two red Audis in Wayside.

I stuffed my fist into my mouth to stifle the scream that welled inside. I wanted to run.

Instead, I marched back into the bedroom, grabbed a pillow, and smacked his head. "You bastard, cheating lying scum!"

"What the hell is wrong with you? Stop hitting me!"

"I will not stop. I have proof. You were with that reporter. You kissed her, then had the nerve to come home and kiss me as if you hadn't had any sex in years. Ugh. To think I believed you all those times when I thought…" Unstoppable tears interrupted my voice.

"Sarah, look, it's not what you think."

That statement was enough to dam the flow. "It's exactly what I think." I sniffled and wiped my nose with my fluffy robe, "I have pictures to prove it."

Derrick had the gall to look embarrassed. Like a little boy caught stealing cookies.

"Out!"

"What?"

I picked up the first thing I could get my hands on. I didn't realize how heavy the brass lamp was until I held it over my head. "Get out. Go to your mother. Go to that bitch. Just get out!"

Derrick didn't argue. He grabbed some clothes from a drawer and ran out.

I printed the picture and then picked Brendan up early from school.

His mother called me the next morning. "Sarah, darling."

I answered but remained mute.

"Dear, I understand you don't want to talk. Derrick told me you had a misunderstanding last night. I am sorry, but all marriages go through these little foibles. The thing is, we need to stick together. I know you are overwrought." She paused and then continued. "Dr. Jansen mentioned to me about your visits. He said you were managing the medication just fine." Another pause. "Perhaps you should go see him again to get an adjustment? Maybe you'd like to drop Brendan off and take a little vacation?"

Medication? Visits? Vacation? I'd never seen Dr. Jansen in my life. I know of him because he was the only psychiatric doctor on staff at the only hospital in town. My confusion cleared instantly when I realized the direction in which she was heading. Dr. Jansen, one of her puppets, would do, write, prescribe, and say anything she wanted.

Her rambling continued but then she rammed her message home. "Derrick needs to be living with his wife, his family. He needs to go home, or I will have to protect poor Brendan from his unstable mother."

I understood the threat, and Derrick returned with his tail between his legs. It wasn't enough, though, to build bridges between the chasm that separated us now. I moved into the guest room.

The whiskey bottles piled up. One night, Derrick stumbled into the guest room and fell on top of me. "C'mon, dahlin', let's do it like we used to?"

It took all my strength to shove him off, and he hit the floor and passed out. I decided to leave the next day. He saw me packing and left the room.

A few minutes later he walked in with his phone. "Sarah, Mother wishes to speak with you."

"I don't want to speak with her."

"Sarah, if you love Brendan, then you will need to take this."

I froze and he handed me the phone.

"Sarah, darling, I'm worried about you. Dr. Jensen assured me that you were making progress, but Derrick just told me what you are doing.

My breath quickened, but I held in my temper.

"Sarah, I know you are listening. I also know about your affair."

My control snapped. "What the hell are you talking about?"

Derrick must have known where this was going, because he handed me an envelope. I opened it and shock waves hit me. There were several photos of a naked woman and a man. You couldn't see the woman's face, but if you didn't know it, you'd think she was me. They were in our bedroom, in our house. Then I realized. The nanny. They must have made these for Margaret.

"Sarah, are you there? Did Derrick show you the pictures?"

"What the hell, they aren't me."

"Oh darling, I know it's hard to admit you are having trouble, but we care about you. But, if you feel you must leave, please know that Brendan will be well cared for."

The message was loud and clear. I couldn't run. The strings held me in place. I started putting my clothes back in the dresser. Derrick took the phone and walked out of the room.

In order to stay with my child, I held my tongue. Now that I knew the stakes, I created every happy moment I could that surrounded Brendan. He loved school, his kindergarten friends, and all the presents Margaret bestowed upon him. I could live with all of it, I thought, as long as Brendan remained happy.

But, a few months later, in mid-summer, she changed everything. She waltzed into the house without knocking and prattled on about the weather and other social events.

"Margaret!" I interrupted coolly. "Why are you here?"

She handed me a brochure announcing the name of a private boarding school. Tall brick buildings and green lawns covered the paper.

"What's this?"

"Brendan has been accepted into Everly Preparatory School."

"But I never applied to this school."

"You didn't have to, darling. As his grandmother, I am authorized to fill out an application for him."

"You want to send my first-grade son to a boarding school somewhere across the state?

I looked up and opened my mouth, but before I could utter a sound she said, "Chapmans always do their primary years at Everly Prep." Her voice, so calm and syrupy, continued. "Why, that's why we get so far ahead of everyone else. He'll start in one month for the fall term." She laid the brochure on the counter and walked out of the house.

I kept calm. When I picked up Brendan from summer camp that afternoon, we went directly home. He whined, but I promised him some fast food burgers and that made him happy. "Let's play a new game," I said throwing his small suitcase onto his king-sized bed with satin sheets. I pointed to his dresser. "How much stuff from your dresser can you fit into there?"

Brendan loved games. He raced back and forth to the drawers randomly pulling things and stuffing them into the suitcase. I grabbed his underwear, socks, and a few pairs of jeans and added it to the pile. I zipped up his bag. "Let's do this in my room, shall we?"

In my bedroom I let him pull things out of my drawers while I packed what I thought I'd need.

We got into my car and drove to the local fast-food joint. I even let Brendan get a milkshake before settling back into the car and driving away. Two miles out of town I relaxed until I heard the siren behind me.

"Shit, shit, shit." I pounded the steering wheel but slowed to a stop on the shoulder. Over the pounding in my head, I heard Brendan gleefully say, "Shit, shit, shit."

The sheriff motioned for me to roll down my window.

"Mrs. Chapman." He tipped his hat.

"Yes, Officer Malone?"

"Please get out of the car and place your hands on the roof."

I was miffed. What the hell was this about? Even a speeding ticket wouldn't have a cop asking me to get out of the car.

"Sir, please tell me what this is about."

"Ma'am, get out of the car."

Another police car pulled in front of mine. I couldn't pull away. I looked back at Brendan, "Honey, I'm going to get out of the car and talk to the nice police officer. I'll be right back."

But when I got out of the car they cuffed me and walked me to the door of their cruiser.

"You can't do this. I have a child in the car. This is not right."

"Ma'am, you will make it a lot easier if you cooperate. We have everything under control. Please calm down."

That's when I saw Margaret sliding out of the cruiser in front of my car followed by Officer Malone. She opened the back door of my car, unhooked Brendan from his car seat, and pulled him from the car. I heard her loud voice. "Brendan, Mommy has to take care of some things. How about a ride in the police car with Grandmother? Do you want to hear the sirens?"

I looked at Officer Malone and sighed, "She's got you too?"

He turned his head but did not answer.

I rubbed my eyes, the cuffs jingling in front of my face. There was nothing I could say at this point. I heard Brendan shout, "Wheee!"

They took me to a private room at the hospital. I didn't resist, but they handcuffed me to the bed frame anyway. The young officer leaned over and whispered, "Sorry," before leaving the room.

After sitting alone for an hour, my bladder was ready to burst.

Dr. Jansen walked in. Clipboard in hand, he rifled through a few pages and then looked toward me. He couldn't look me in the eye but stared at my neck and my breasts.

"Mrs. Chapman." He cleared his throat, "It appears you've had a nervous breakdown. I will prescribe some antidepressants and some sleep aids." A nurse came in with a syringe.

"What's in there?" I asked.

The nurse pushed the plunger a bit to let the air bubbles out. "It's Midazolam. It will help you relax."

"I don't want it! You don't have the right. You can't give it to me!" I yelled and backed up but I couldn't go very far.

The nurse looked at Dr. Jansen and he nodded his head. She lowered the syringe and slowly walked up to me. "You'll be fine. Let's sit down and we can talk about it."

"I have to use the restroom."

The nurse pointed to a door.

After relieving myself, I took a moment to think. I had to play along, but I was not going to take medicine. I opened the door. "Okay, let's talk."

As soon as I sat on the bed, she stuck the needle into my shoulder. "There, you should feel better soon."

The drugs overtook me and I slumped back onto the bed. A police officer entered the room and removed my cuffs, but I couldn't care less at that point. I couldn't think or do anything. I closed my eyes and slept.

I woke sometime in the middle of the night. A couple of nurses came in and I pretended to sleep. I heard one say, "You look so tired. Here, this is her evening dose. It might help you sleep. She doesn't need it. She's still out cold."

After they left, I sat up. I briefly wondered what kind of strings Margaret had tied to Dr. Jenson. He seemed like a nice guy, but he definitely did not direct his own life.

My brain cleared since I missed the dose of medicine. That shot paralyzed me. I didn't want any more of that. But how could I avoid it?

In the dim light, I read the dosing schedule on my chart, then I had an idea. I found a used needle and filled it with water. My hope was to distract the nurse and switch the syringes.

I couldn't believe how easy it was. When the nurse left, I hid the drug-filled syringe in a paper towel in my sneaker.

I went back to the bed and pretended to sleep. I was unable to escape the midday dose and slept until evening. I woke to Derrick's beautiful but soulless eyes.

"Hello, Sarah."

I turned my head away from him. "Derrick?"

"You really should learn to cooperate with Mother. I hate seeing you here like this. I know we have our problems, but will you at least try to see things Mother's way?"

I seethed inside. My body felt lethargic, but my brain felt the explosions. I wanted to hit him. Instead, I nodded my head and mumbled, "It's for the best."

He smiled. That damn son-of-a bitch smiled. "There's a good girl. I knew you'd come around."

He took my hand. I let it hang heavy in his. "I'll tell Mother this evening and we can have you out of here by tomorrow."

Shortly after he left, the evening nurse came in with another, inescapable syringe. I fell asleep knowing that the one in the middle of the night would not reach me.

In the morning, I told the nurse I was being discharged, and that I would not need the shot. She left the syringe on the bedside table and left to confer with the doctor. I quickly made another switch as I had done before. She returned looking none too happy. "You won't be leaving until after dinner." She grabbed the syringe and almost stabbed it into my arm. The water formed little bubbles under my skin. The nurse glanced at it, frowning. She shrugged and left the room.

That evening, Derrick picked me up. How sweet, he brought me a fresh outfit, a drab skirt, slippers, and a T-shirt, probably picked by Margaret to humiliate me.

I stuffed my dirty clothes into a plastic bag, hiding the syringes with the drugs.

Instead of taking me home, he took me to Mother's. I cringed but realized that this might be for the best. It would give me time to plan what I needed to do.

At first, I avoided Margaret, saying how sleepy the pills made me. I took pains to seem sleepy while I played with Brandon and went to bed right after he did. After a few days, I started having tea with Margaret.

I had to be careful to always remain calm, as if slightly fuzzy-headed. Margaret was keen to observe me and smiled indulgently, knowingly, as I kissed her heavily made-up cheek goodnight. Then I'd put Brendan to bed and go to my own.

More sedatives went down the toilet, and each night I stayed in bed thinking and planning. The two syringes of Midazolam were my loaded guns, my secret weapons. But I worried, though I hid them well, that they would be found and disposed of by the maids.

August arrived and I asked Margaret if Brendan and I could spend time at their small cabin in the mountains. "You know, before he goes off to school at Everly?"

Margaret refused to let me drive Brendan anywhere. "For safety reasons," she said. I hoped she would agree and drive us there, but she surprised me with her response. "Let's plan to stay a few days." Seeing the shock on my face she added, "You see, Sarah, I'm not as bad as you think."

The cabin, though more of a chateau, stood under tall trees in the mountains about ten miles from the interstate. The four bedrooms, a fully stocked kitchen, vaulted ceilings, and a sauna off the back deck exuded wealth and privilege.

Margaret watched TV, spoke to countless people on her phone, and arranged for in-home spa treatments. The poor masseuse traveled over an hour to provide her services.

Brendan and I walked by the small shed to a trail that led into the woods. He delighted in seeing deer in the mornings and rabbits running across the road. The peaceful moments almost made me forget my plans.

Almost.

The day before our return home, I suggested to Margaret that we take Brendan to the small zoo, just a few miles past the bridge. She agreed. I gathered my large purse which carried extra clothes and a water bottle for Brendan. It also carried the needles from the hospital. Into my pocket, I dropped a couple of the antidepressants. They wouldn't put Margaret to sleep, but I hoped they might make her feel dizzy. I didn't want her to fall asleep. I wanted her to see what was coming.

After walking for an hour and visiting all the animals, I suggested we allow Brendan to eat something at the zoo's small restaurant. Margaret hesitated slightly, but Brendan pleaded and she gave in.

I wondered if Margaret would ever use the bathroom. She hadn't used one all morning. But finally, she excused herself to go. I quickly added the sleeping pills to her coffee, then stirred it with the spoon until the white specks disappeared.

She sat down with a flourish. It took everything I had not to look at her coffee cup. When I saw it hit her lips I grabbed Brendan's hand and squeezed it. I needed to remind myself what was at stake.

"Why'd you do that, Mommy?"

"Because I love you. This has been fun, hasn't it?"

Margaret set her cup down and I noticed it was almost all gone. I felt my shoulders relax.

I ordered a huge salad and let Brendan order a few things as well. I needed time for the pills to start working.

After about thirty minutes, I noticed Margaret touching her head.

"Is something wrong?" I asked in my most concerned voice?

"I'm not feeling so well. Perhaps we should leave."

"Okay." I looked at Brendan. "Dear, Grandmother is not feeling well. We need to gather our food and leave."

"Will she go in the hospital like you did?"

"I don't think so. Let's get her back to the cabin, okay?"

"Okay."

He helped by carrying Margaret's purse to the car. When Margaret tried to get behind the wheel, I suggested that I drive.

She peered at me, then finally nodded. "I suppose it's for the best. I don't know what has come over me."

Margaret flopped into the car, something she would never do. Time for the next part.

I hooked Brendan into his car seat and slid behind the wheel. After a mile or so, Brendan fell asleep. I pulled onto the shoulder.

"Why're we stoppin'?" Margaret asked in a slurred voice.

"I want to get a blanket to put on top of Brendan. The A/C is cold."

"That's good." Margaret closed her eyes.

I reached into my large bag and retrieved the syringe of Midazolam. Margaret didn't see it coming. When the needle punctured her shoulder, she yelped. Her eyes blinked rapidly, fear creeping in.

"Whad was thad?" she mumbled.

"Nothing to worry about, Margaret," I said in my sweetest voice.

I pulled back onto the road and drove around until her head flopped over. Drool came out of her lips. Paralysis ensued. I headed to the cabin.

Her eyes followed me as I carried the still-sleeping Brendan into the cabin. Confident that Brendan would sleep for another hour or more, I kissed his cheek and then turned on all the lights in case he woke before I returned. I locked the doors so he couldn't go anywhere.

In the car, I cupped Margaret's chin and turned her head toward me. I smiled. "How does it feel, Margaret?"

She couldn't respond. When I let go of her chin, her head flopped onto her chest.

I cranked the engine. "Do you feel like a puppet?"

I stepped on the gas and drove the two miles to the bridge. No cars were visible when I stopped in the middle.

Thankfully, Margaret weighed little, but her limp body made pulling her out of the car difficult. She made grunting noises while I pulled her feet out of the wheel well and turned her torso so it faced me.

"What's wrong, Margaret? Cat got your tongue?"

I turned my back to her belly and knelt down. I pulled her hands around my neck, then stood, carrying her piggyback style. Her feet dragged on the asphalt as I made my way to the bridge's railing. I twisted our bodies so that she fell against the rail and heaved her upper torso so it leaned halfway over, her arms dangling at her sides. Her head dripped on the other side, much like a wet towel on a rack.

I kept my hand on her back so she wouldn't slip off the railing. After checking again to make sure we were alone, I knelt down so I could look at her upside-down face. I saw terror in her eyes.

Briefly I questioned myself. If I stopped now, would she remember? Would anything change?

I took another look around, then looked hard into Margaret's eyes. "You make a good puppet, Margaret. The best kind, quiet and nimble."

I stood, grabbed her hands, and threw her floppy arms over the railing. They fell, jiggling by her ears. Next, I grabbed her ankles and lifted them higher and higher until gravity did its job.

I made it home before Brendan woke from his nap. Hours later, after walking, playing, and swimming in the hot tub filled with bubbles, Brendan asked, "Where's Margaret?"

Not Grandma, Granny, or MiMi, but Margaret. I shrugged. "A nice gentleman came in a car and picked her up. She said she had errands to run."

After the bubble bath, we watched TV and I let him watch anything he wanted. We snuggled in my king-sized bed until he fell asleep.

With his sleeping, strawberry-scented body nestled into mine, I waited. I waited for guilt to overtake me. I waited for remorse to visit me. But peace, only peace, entered my soul and I drifted off to sleep.

I woke around three in the morning. Her purse! I needed to throw it into the river. Brendan still slept. I turned all the lights on again and drove back to the bridge. I debated pulling out the three hundred dollars in cash but realized then it might look like a robbery. I didn't want that. I didn't want them searching for someone. I took out a few twenties for lunch on the way home and left the rest in her wallet.

They found her body four days later. The purse was never found.

The funeral took place a month later. I had no interest in planning it, and

Derrick took a few weeks to recover before he let the funeral home make all the plans. I knew he was fine though when the bimbo reporter moved in with him.

I didn't want to go but thought of Brendan. Maybe he needed to see this to have closure. He liked Margaret and was probably the only person who did.

Once the coffin made it into the ground, people walked up to me offering their condolences. I had a hard time telling if they were heartfelt. But the Sheriff approached me, took my hand, and said something odd. "It's better this way." He palmed two folded sheets of paper into my hand, leaned in, and kissed my cheek.

I couldn't read them right away because Brendan started crying when he saw his daddy hug the Bimbo. I stuffed them in my purse.

After the reading of her will, the town relaxed. Derrick inherited most of the estate except a portion put into a trust for Brendan. I received nothing from her, but got a boatload in my divorce. Though the state of Virginia usually required one year of separation before filing for a divorce, the Circuit Court Judge, after a private interview with the Sheriff, happily granted me one. Uncontested.

Derrick signed all parental rights over to me. I was free to do as I wished. With no idea where to go, I asked Brendan what he wanted to do.

"I want to be a cowboy."

We moved to Texas, bought a small house with some land, and filled up the empty paddocks with a large pony and some goats.

I had nightmares for a while. That she wasn't dead. That the body they found wasn't hers and she would steal Brendan from the house in the middle of the night. Sometimes I dreamed that they would discover what really happened and put me in jail. That I'd lose Brendan anyway because of her.

Then. after a particularly vivid dream where I slammed her coffin shut, I woke with the realization that I never looked at those papers from the Sheriff.

I dug through some unpacked boxes until I found the purse from the funeral and pulled out the papers.

The first was a copy of the coroner's report. It reported traces of Midazolam and other antidepressants in her bloodstream. Written under the manner of death were the words "Anomic suicide." Written under the cause of death was one word: Drowned.

I opened the other paper and in the middle of a plain sheet was a sticky note that simply said, "We are all free. Thank you."

A tumor will grow and fester

It will leach your energy

It will cripple your heart

Before it engulfs you

Before you loose your soul

Cut it out

Magic in Memories

Brotherly Love

*B*arry's mom handed him a few sugar cubes saying, "Go outside and take your brother with you!"

Argh, Barry hated it when his mom said that. The last thing he wanted to do was play with Joey. He'd rather eat spinach. Joey ruined everything when he was born, and ever since Dad died, Barry was stuck with him. All the time.

But he had to listen to his mom or he'd get in trouble. He pocketed the sugar and pulled his brother off the couch. "C'mon."

They walked the familiar trail in the woods that led to their backyard campsite. Barry liked playing computer games. He liked staying clean. He'd rather put all his clothes away than play outside, especially in this heat.

His brother, Joey, ran from tree to tree looking for bugs. Barry hated bugs. Joey asked him questions all the time. "What's this tree? Why is shade cooler? When will this caterpillar turn into a butterfly?" On and on, Joey never stopped. Most times, Barry had no clue what to answer except for, "We'll look it up when we get back inside." Still, even with the same evasive answer, Joey always asked.

Joey stopped to gaze up at the huge pecan tree. Barry looked up too. The tree was wider than Barry could stretch both his arms. The roots were tangled among the blades of grass like noodles in spaghetti and meatball sauce. Dad used to say it guarded the campsite.

The thought of Dad hurt. Barry didn't want to be reminded. "Let's go back, Joe. It's too hot to play."

"Barry, look!" Joey pointed and then ran to a spot between the roots. "It's a nest! It must have fallen from the tree."

Barry dutifully knelt down next to his brother. Small twigs and leaves formed a braided circle in the hollow space between the roots. Barry didn't know anything about nests except for the ones he saw in pictures. But those were made of twigs and mud and looked like a small bowl. He didn't think this round twiggy thing was a nest. But then what did he know? It did have something like an egg in the middle.

Barry wondered if it was an egg or just a weird rock. It looked almost like one of those big marbles from his marble set.

Barry reached for it, but before he could move too close, Joey slapped his hand out of the way. "Don't touch it!"

"Shut up, Joe, it's just a rock."

"It might be an egg. Mama said not to touch bird eggs."

"Joe, I know what Mama said, I've heard her say it for four years more than you have, but, does this look like an egg to you?"

Joey studied it a while and then sighed. "No, I guess not."

Barry lifted the marble-like stone from the nest. For once, he felt curious. The rock was bigger than his marble shooter but smaller than a golf ball. It felt like the rocks along the lake where the water washed over the sand. Smooth and round.

"Can we keep it?" Joey reached for the rock.

Barry pulled his hand away. "Let it alone, Joey. You can't always have everything!"

He brought it back down so he could look at it. As it sat in his open palm, tiny blue and green specks formed around it like clouds blowing in the wind. He closed his fingers. Warmth traveled into his heart. He closed his eyes and felt happy, like jumping on a bed, eating ice cream, or even getting a hug from his dad.

Then he saw him. "Dad, is that you? I thought Mama said you were in heaven."

Memories flooded his brain. He and his dad getting ice cream, trying to camp under the stars, and getting rained on. He remembered the time he threw up all over his dad's computer. Dad didn't care about the mess. He hugged Barry and told him everything would be all right.

He remembered Dad holding baby Joey and saying, "Barry, this is your little brother. He'll be your friend for life if you let him be. We're going to have so much fun together."

But there never was any fun. Joey always cried and Dad ignored Barry to sing to Joey. Gone were the camping days, and the ice cream runs to the store.

Then his father left. Mom said it was an accident, but Barry blamed it on Joey 'cause Joey wouldn't stop crying.

"Dad, come back. I miss you!"

A few more memories appeared, clear as day. Dad, Barry, and baby Joey watching cartoons. Barry on his bike racing Dad while Dad pushed Joey in the stroller. Baby Joey laughing while stuffed in a backpack carrier while Barry and Dad made pancakes for mom. Flour went everywhere, including all over Joey's bald head.

His father opened his mouth but Barry couldn't hear anything.

Then, ever so softly, he heard his name. He thought his dad called out to him, but then he realized it was the voice of his little brother growing louder in his ears.

"Barry, Barry, wake up! You can't die. I love you!"

He lifted his eyelids to see his brother standing over him. Tears streamed down Joey's cheeks. "Huh? What happened?"

Joey dove in to give Barry a bear hug. "You're alive!"

"Of course I'm alive. But what happened?"

Joey sniffed and wiped his nose with the back of his hand. "I think you fainted or something. I don't know, it was strange. You closed your eyes and then sunk onto the grass. You know, like when your sugar goes low. But you didn't fall fast like you usually do, it was like, slow motion or something."

"How long was I out?"

"Forever. I yelled your name a lot. I remembered the sugar cube and stuck it in your mouth. I was about to go get Mama but then you said something so I waited."

"What did I say?"

"I'm not sure."

"Well, give me an idea anyway."

"You said something like, "Kay, I'll watch.""

Barry noticed the rock in his hand. A few specks of green and blue dust dotted his palm. The rock felt cool. He gently placed the rock back in the round nest.

He wiped his hands to remove the rest of the dust, "That was weird." He looked around the campsite. He didn't feel angry now. He noted the sun on the horizon. "We should get home, it's late."

"But what about the rock, can we keep it?"

"I don't think so. Somebody could have put it there for a reason and we wouldn't want to take someone else's things, would we?"

"I guess not. I'll race you home!"

Joey did not expect Barry to react. Normally, Barry would say, "Go," and then walk home letting Joey get there way ahead of him.

But that's not what Barry did. He said, "Okay, champ, you better run fast. The last one home is a rotten egg!"

The boys took off, running on the forest trail back to their house. Barry let Joey win, that's what Dad used to do for Barry, but he made it a real race.

Back at the tree, among the gnarly branches, a beautiful fairy peeked out to watch the boys run off. When they disappeared from sight, the four-inch-tall fairy stood and stretched her still-growing wings. Translucent, spidery wings fluffed out like a butterfly. She pulled her long, black hair free from a twig, crossed her arms, then smiled.

Her duties as guardian hadn't fully started yet, but with the help of the stone, she'd brought peace to the older brother.

Thankful that the boys didn't take the rock, she climbed into the nest, looked up, and sent an air kiss toward heaven. "Thank you, Dad. I should be able to take over from here."

She lay on top of the rock. Green and blue specks of dust rose up and formed a cloud. It swirled until both the fairy and the rock disappeared into the tree.

Embracing Christmas

Hopeful, Community Love

*P*eople in little towns always talk. Just a few wrong words, spoken at the wrong time, can change everything.

Everybody knew everybody in Lowell City. They called it a city but it wasn't really a city, just a bunch of old buildings on Main Street. On the east side, in the middle, was the town hall made of faded bricks. The downstairs windows had bars on them. Mama used to point to them and say, "Mind your manners or they'll put you behind bars."

On the north side of town hall sat three old, white, wooden houses with peeling paint. The porches, dotted with old rocking chairs and wicker tables, went all around the houses like skirts. How I wished I lived in one of those.

The Five & Dime, the best store ever, took up the south side of town hall. You could get almost anything there. The huge glass windows in the front were like portals to a holiday-themed fantasy world.

Across the street from the Five & Dime stood a gas station with two red pumps. Stretched out on one side of the gas station, a bunch of small shops of different sizes and colors looked like a variety of shoe boxes sitting side by side. On the other side of the gas station the grocery store announced sales on bread and milk.

Before you went in to take advantage of the sales, you had to pass one of those mechanical horses that kids loved to ride. It never worked, but I loved pretending. I'd bounce up and down and yell, "Yee ha!"

That is, until the sad day when Mama said, "Sophie, you are too big for that wooden horse." I used to get a teensy bit jealous when my little sister rode it.

My daddy, Daddy Bo, used to be the high school football hero, or so they said. Everybody loved him. I couldn't go anywhere without hearing the same story over and over about how he, the best quarterback in Lowell City's history, took the high school team to the West Virginia State Championships. They had high hopes for Daddy Bo.

Mama met Daddy Bo in her senior year of high school after the county combined two schools. Mama always said, "The minute I walked into Mrs. Farnsworth's homeroom, I fell in love."

Even though Daddy Bo could have gone to college on a football scholarship, he didn't. Instead, Daddy Bo and Mama got married. Daddy Bo got a job with a trucking company. People were a little sore that he didn't go to college. His Mama, Granny Em, was especially mad. He was, after all, supposed to put Lowell City on the map. I never understood that, I thought it was already on the map.

Anyhow, Granny Em and Bo's daddy, Grandpa Joe, didn't want anything to do with Mama. They used to ask Bo to visit the farm when he was leaving town or coming back from a run. They were as cool as ice around Mama.

That all changed a year later when I came along. Everyone got happier. Bo would sing in the choir. On Christmas morning he would pull me on the sled, all over town, yelling, "Merry Christmas!" to everyone. Mama and Daddy Bo were always smiling.

Granny Em and Grandpa Joe must have melted a little. I can remember going to the farm after church on Christmas Day. I remember chasing chickens and eating pie. I don't see them now.

When I turned six, Sammy came along. Sammy never knew Daddy Bo 'cause he died just before she was born. He got killed in a trucking accident just around Christmas. That was the saddest time ever. I don't remember opening any presents that year but I remember the sadness.

Mama looked to Granny Em and Grandpa Joe for help but didn't get any. Mama says, "They were so sad they got frozen in it." Granny Em and Grandpa Joe sold their farm and left. Like I said, I don't see them now.

Mama had to work since we didn't have any money. Granny May, Mama's Mama, came for a while to help with Sammy. She and Mama fought all the time and after Sammy turned six months, Granny May left. Mama said it was better that way. Now her hard-earned money could be spent on us instead of Granny's booze. I was only six and didn't really know what "booze" was, but if Mama said it was so, then it was so.

It was just before Christmas, a year later, that Mama stopped taking us to church. People meant well, I know. They missed my daddy too, but they reminded Mama all the time that he was gone. They said things like, "I wish Daddy Bo could be here." Then there were the sad sighs that came along with, "Daddy Bo was such a good singer." They were always reminding me that I was "the spitting image of your Daddy Bo." While this was certainly true and Mama said it all the time, having other people reminding us about it made us sadder.

What really led Mama to leave the church, though, wasn't so much the reminders. It was the conversations. The ones they didn't think we could hear. The voices that suddenly stopped when we entered a room. The whispers as we passed by.

Mama overheard two ladies, old friends of Granny Em's, talking one day. They said, "It's a darn shame how she chased Em and Joe away."

"I know. Did you hear that Bo didn't have to go out that day, but that she made him go? The roads were too icy!"

They blamed Mama for Daddy Bo's death? Mama was outraged. She had begged Daddy Bo not to go, not to take that last truckload. Mama, too proud to say anything to defend herself, quietly turned and walked out of the church.

Mama had been hanging by her fingers on a cliff all year and the grief she felt was pulling her down. For Mama, their words sent her off the edge into the frozen water. She was just too sad to deal with it. We didn't go back to the church after that.

We were missed that Christmas. I was supposed to be in a Christmas pageant. My friend Torrie told me later that the choir director had to say my lines. The pastor came by a few times after that, but all Mama did was smile sadly and shake her head. Then the busybodies came by on their charity missions, but Mama always shooed them away with a, "No thank you," as polite as she could. After a few months, even they stopped coming by.

Once you start avoiding people, you got to stay away. People want reasons and apologies. They want you to talk about why you didn't come back. Mama could not swallow her pride and admit she needed help. We stayed to ourselves when we could.

Without the free clothes and food from the church, we had to scrimp and save even more. The next few Christmases were slim. Mama did her best. She wasn't a grinch, but, as far as I could tell, other people were thinking that she was.

While other kids were getting skateboards and new bikes, Sammy and I were getting thrift store clothes, toys, and knit hats. It was embarrassing, so I stopped talking about what I got for Christmas. It's easy to not say anything when your friends can't stop talking about themselves. But sometimes I'd get the look. The one that said, "Poor little Sophie!" I ran from that look.

I think Mama was embarrassed too but she never talked about it. In order to afford a decent dinner and the few things we got, Mama skimped on decorations. We had a paper tree that I made in school taped to the refrigerator. The stuff I made in school was all we had. On Christmas morning, our "useful" gifts were in two neat piles on the kitchen table.

Mama worked at the gas station right off Highway 13. Too many church folks went to the one in town. Mama said the highway station paid better anyway. Plus, the manager, Mr. Barton, let her bring home the chicken and other food that they would normally throw away. I never did get tired of that yummy, crispy chicken.

Being poor wasn't a choice, it was just the way it was. I loved playing in the river rather than the private pool. I had some friends who didn't care that I lived in a trailer park and would hang out with me in the library or play ball with me in the park. I didn't mind playing with my little sister, she was fun. But the older I got, the more I felt it, especially at Christmas. I sometimes felt that the world had forgotten our little family. I understood why we did things the way we did, but I wanted more. Wasn't this the time to forgive, to give, and to make others happy?

I look back now and think how some harmful words that my Mama wasn't supposed to hear changed the direction of our lives. Yet I also remember how a few words we didn't hear opened Mama's heart.

It was the last day of school before Christmas break. The bus dropped me off at the corner where Sammy went to the babysitter. Normally I'd wait with Sammy at the babysitter's house so Mama could pick both of us up, but today Mama said I could walk the two blocks home. I had a key to the trailer and was going to spend a whole hour by myself for the first time ever.

As I walked, I noticed how Christmas covered the town. Green wreaths with red bows dotted the doorways. Lamp posts were wrapped in ribbon. Santa rang a bell in front of the grocery store. Christmas songs floated into the streets getting louder as people opened doors.

I smiled at my reflection in the Five & Dime's window. A fat snowman with a bad haircut stared back at me. My winter coat was huge. A green woolen scarf wrapped around my neck, and a blue bubble cap sat on my head. My unruly brown hair stuck out at all angles and my nose turned pink from the cold.

Beyond my reflection, a toy train chugged around its tracks. The train went in and out of tunnels and passed little villages lined with plastic trees. Round and round it went. I'd love to have a train. I'd love to have a Christmas tree for it to go around.

Here I was, ten years old, with a whole hour to do anything I wanted, and all I did was stare at things I couldn't have. I brought a few library books home, but I could read them later after Sammy fell asleep.

As I continued staring into the window, ungracious thoughts ran through my head. I was tired of being sad. I was tired of my mama being sad. I was tired of pretending our little "at-home Christmas" was okay.

"God, if you're up there," I said to myself, "could you tell Daddy Bo that I wish he was still here? Mama and I miss him. I miss going to church and I miss the fun we had."

Perhaps he was listening, for the strangest thing happened.

While watching the train go around and around, I almost screamed when a strange man with blue eyes and blond hair sticking out of his black cap tapped my shoulder.

"I'm sorry. I didn't mean to scare you. My name is Mr. Tash and I'm running late. I have to fill up my car since it won't make the next thirty miles without gas and I need to buy a present for my soon-to-be stepdaughter. I have no idea what little girls want, but you're about her age. Would you mind buying some things for her while I get gas? You'd save me loads of time."

I bristled a little bit about being called a "little" girl but nodded my head. Mr. Tash handed me three crisp twenty-dollar bills, then ran across the street to the gas station and opened the gas cap on a sleek black Mercedes.

I turned and went into the store. I bought what I would have wanted. Along with a bottle of perfume, a pearl-handled brush, and a pair of fluffy pink earmuffs, I picked out a beautiful red silk scarf. At the counter were some chocolate toffee bars, so I threw those in the pile as well.

Mr. Matthews, the shopkeeper, raised his eyebrows when I plunked the sixty dollars on the counter but he calmly asked, "Sophie, do you want to get a gift bag to put this in?"

"How much more will that be, Mr. Matthews?"

"It's a dollar."

"I think there is enough."

"There is plenty."

I walked out the door just as the man came out of the gas station. He ran over to me and said, "Dear, I can't thank you enough!" He took the bag of stuff I handed to him. He didn't look at it. I held out the leftover cash but he pushed it back toward me.

"Oh no, you earned it. I would have been really late if I did it. I'm already in the doghouse for not getting there sooner."

He swiftly walked to his car, got in with a wave, and drove away.

There, in my hands, I counted nineteen dollars and some change. I walked back into the store and stared at the perfume and makeup. I gazed longingly at the other items on the shelf, then shoved the money into my coat pocket and ran out of the store. I ran and ran, not paying attention to where I was going.

My brain took me to the park by the river. I felt comfortable there and could think. I didn't like my thoughts much. If money could be a weight, then I was carrying a million pounds in my pocket. I kept thinking that I could spend it all and Mama and Sammy would never know.

Patches of ice drifted slowly around a bend in the river. In much the same manner, an awareness of how this little bit of money could give me, Mama, and Sammy a nicer Christmas flowed into my head.

But then a wave of anger bubbled up. Why should I share this money? I shook the money in the air and yelled to the chunks of ice, "I earned this!"

The soft sound of gurgling water whispered, "Do the right thing."

Though thoughts of what I should do were ringing in my ears, I ignored them. With my mind made up, I purposefully walked back into town.

I opened the door to the Five & Dime and filled a basket with whatever I wanted. Each plop of an item into the basket was like the sound of a BB hitting a stop sign. If you've never shot a BB gun at a metal sign, you are missing out. Somewhere in my brain was the thought, "Will I get into trouble like I did shooting the sign?"

My thoughts got too loud for my body and I reminded myself, "But it is my money. I earned it!"

"Who are you talking to?" asked Mr. Matthews.

"Nobody, just thinking out loud."

I finished adding some of the chocolate toffees to my basket and placed it on the counter. Mr. Matthews added it up and it was too much stuff. With a forced grin, I put back the bottle of perfume saying to myself, "I didn't want to smell like a bunch of lilacs anyway."

With all my goodies loaded into a bag and shoved into my satchel, I made my way home. I was working on a story to explain it all, though I didn't really need a story. I was working on one anyway to tell Mama why I got so much stuff when I noticed her car in the driveway. There was a police car there too.

This can't be good. I ran into the trailer just as the Sheriff was leaving. "Let us know if you need anything."

"What's wrong?" I asked.

"Hello, Sophie. I'll tell you while we go pick up Sammy. Come on, let's walk and go get her."

We trekked back into town. Mama was quiet for a bit. I knew not to push her since that would only make her not tell me. The crunch of snow grew louder while the guilt I felt about the money grew heavier. Then Mama spoke.

"I'm home early from the gas station because Mr. Barton told me to leave."

"What, you're fired?"

Mama wrinkled her nose. "No, nothing like that, but I needed a little break. Everything is okay, but the store was robbed."

"Robbed? Who did it? Are you okay?"

"Yes, I'm fine, just a little shaken. He took all the money in the drawer and my wallet too."

"Oh no." My voice drifted off.

"We'll be fine, Sophie. Don't you worry. We'll just have to hold back on presents this year.”

I couldn’t say a thing. The bag I was carrying might as well have been strangling me.

“Mama?”

“Yes?”

“I’m sorry.”

“It’s not your fault.”

We passed the Five & Dime and my heart was torn. “How can I be so stingy?” I thought to myself. An idea popped into my brain and I chewed on it a while.

We got to the babysitter’s and picked up Sammy, then started walking home. Sammy chatted on and on about her day, the snowman she made, and the snacks she had. She didn’t notice how quiet the two older people were.

On the way back, as we neared the Five & Dime, I said, “Mama, can you wait here a minute?”

“What for?”

“I got to do something, just please wait a minute?”

“Okay, but don’t be long, it’s too cold for Sammy to be just standing out here.”

“I won’t.”

I ran into the store and looked at Mr. Matthews.

“Hello, Sophie, what brings you back here? I heard what happened at the station, is your Mama okay?”

“Yes, sir, I think so, but I need the money back.”

Mr. Matthews frowned. “I’m so sorry. Sure, no problem.”

I put the bag on the counter and Mr. Matthews gave me back the cash. With a wave of relief, I stuffed it into my pocket and ran back outside.

“What was that all about?”

“I’ll tell you at home.”

I put the money on the kitchen counter and told Mama the story. She didn’t believe me at first.

“You can call Mr. Matthews and ask him!” I said.

She sat quietly on a stool, then softly said, “No need. I believe you. You didn’t have to put the stuff back, we will be okay.”

“I didn’t feel right spending it.”

She continued to sit quietly while I started to help Sammy take off her clunky winter clothes.

There was a knock at the door. Mama looked up to see Sheriff Reynolds through the glass. “I wonder why he’s back?” she mused aloud. I froze and left Sammy with her coat hanging lopsided on one arm.

Mama invited Sheriff Reynolds inside. He smiled at everyone.

"I have good news. The burglar was caught trying to buy a beer at the Roadside Cafe. He was so stupid. He pulled out your pink wallet. It's been all over the news that your pink wallet was stolen. Ray called us right away. The rest of the money was stuffed in the mask he used and thrown in his back seat." The Sheriff pulled Mama's wallet from a bag and handed it over.

Mama took the wallet and looked at the cash. A tear was forming in the corner of her eye.

"Let me know if anything's missing. We got a fund for this at the precinct."

Mama looked up and smiled. "Thank you, Sheriff. I believe it's all here."

"Well, if you need anything, just let me know."

"I will. Thank you."

Sheriff Reynolds hesitated, then turned and left. I started tugging at Sammy's coat again.

"Stop!" Mama yelled.

Both Sammy and I looked at her with confused expressions painted on our faces.

"How would you two like to go for a pizza?"

When Sammy heard the question, her big brown eyes widened with hope. It would be her first trip to the pizza shop.

I thought a moment, then my eyes lit too. "We could use the money I got," I said.

"Nonsense! I got my money back. Mr. Barton gave me a Christmas bonus, in cash. What do you say to us having a little more fun this Christmas? We can even go for ice cream."

Ice cream sounded magical.

Sammy and I ran for the door banging into each other as we did. Once outside, we held hands and giggled our way into town. Closer to Sal's Pizza, Mama told Sammy to run ahead. She was so little, and her bulky black winter coat and snow pants made her bobble like a penguin. We laughed even more. Mama's smile made it to her eyes. She sure was pretty when she was happy.

We found an empty table and Betty, a lady that used to sing with Daddy in the choir, smiled at us and walked to our table. "Well, hello there, what brings you out on this cold winter night?"

Sammy's face lit up and she said, "We're having fun for Christmas!"

Betty looked at Mama. "Well, I bet Daddy Bo is smiling down from heaven to see you having a Christmas party. What can I get you?"

I thought for sure that Mama would grow sad at the mention of Daddy Bo, but all she did was nod and say, "Yes, he probably is."

Betty took our order. We opted for the twelve-dollar pepperoni pizza special with extra cheese.

"And what would you girls like to drink."

I lowered my head, feeling guilty for spending money. "Water, please."

Mama covered my hands and laughed. "We'll get three root beers please."

Betty smiled and turned back toward the kitchen. I watched her say something to Sal behind the ovens. I figured she was telling him what we wanted. He started smiling and gesturing and Betty was nodding.

The pizza, unlike those rubbery frozen ones, tasted like pure heaven melted with cheese. I noticed that Mama didn't eat much and I guess that was good because Sammy and I stuffed our faces. After leaving a tip for Betty, we headed to the ice cream shop. Sheriff Reynolds entered the pizza shop while we were leaving. He tipped his hat at us, staring hard at Mama and said, "I'm glad you are doing all right. It's good to see such beautiful, smiling faces!"

Mama paused and said, "Thank you, Sheriff. It's about time we put the spirit back into our lives."

Sammy grabbed Mama's hand. "C'mon, I want ice cream."

Mama smiled at Sheriff Reynolds. "Gotta go!"

In the ice cream shop, I tamped down my excitement. We had already spent too much money.

Mama asked me what I wanted.

"Nothing, I'm full."

"Nonsense, I've got enough left to get some ice cream for the two of you."

"But, Mama, you should get some. It will help you feel better."

"I'm feeling fine. I'd rather buy something at the Five & Dime."

"Okay," I said sheepishly. We took a few minutes to help Sammy pick out a flavor.

Mr. Carson looked concerned. "I heard about the robbery. I'm glad everything is all right. Here you go, little lady!" He handed the ice cream cone to Sammy. "Now what can I get you two ladies?"

We shook our heads.

Mr. Carson's eyes twinkled. "Nonsense, you all get a cone free tonight."

Mama was about to tell Mr. Carson, "No thanks" when he spoke again.

"You three are the twelfth customers to come in today. I'm doing a Twelve Days of Christmas promotion. Every twelfth customer, or family, gets a free cone. Look, see the sign?"

Sure enough, in big red letters, so big I'm surprised we missed them, was a sign with peppermint-colored cones singing the Twelve Days of Christmas. The red letters proclaimed, "Free Cone for Every Twelfth Customer."

Mama smiled. I don't think I ever saw her smile so much. She sang, "On the first day of Christmas my true love gave to me, three ice cream cones for my girls." It didn't sound right because she stretched the words to fit. We all laughed. She wrapped her arms around me and gave her order. "I'll take a pistachio cream in a waffle cone please."

When she thought I wasn't looking, Mama looked up at Mr. Carson, smiled, and mouthed a "thank you." I got the feeling that we were not the twelfth customer that day, but who was I to complain? My rocky road tasted great, Sammy now had rainbow cheeks, and Mom closed her eyes every time she took a lick of her pistachio cream.

With our stomachs full and faces sticky from melted ice cream, we donned our winter gear and walked out of the shop.

Mama clapped her hands together with excitement. "Okay, let's go to the Five & Dime."

Just before we entered, she gave each of us a five-dollar bill. I shook my head, "I don't need it, I have the other money."

Again, Mama turned on her shiny smile. "Take it. It's Christmas."

"Thanks," I said and took the bill. Sammy cheered and skipped her way into the store. Now she looked like one of those bouncing balls that bounced on the words to songs in videos.

It was almost closing time when we walked in. At the counter, a young boy with olive skin and short little fingers was placing quarters in a precise row on the counter. He wore a coat that was about two sizes too big, had a worn cap, and a black scarf. Mr. Matthews was calmly saying, "Now, Randall, you only have seventy-five cents and this here plane is a dollar. You'll have to pick something different."

Randall pouted. "But I want the plane. Mom says if I work real hard, I can earn what I want. I took a wagon load of newspapers to the recycle center and washed all the dishes so I should get the plane."

Mama and I looked at each other. I knew what she was thinking, because I was thinking the same thing. I waved the five-dollar bill and silently signaled to Mr. Matthews, "I got this!"

Mr. Matthews understood but shook his head. He bent over the counter and said to little Randall, "I tell you what, Randall. If you go over there and get that broom for me and push that snow out the door, you will earn the rest of the money for your plane."

Randall's eyes lit up. He tore across the room, brushed the snow out as well as any seven-year-old could, and put the broom back where he found it. He ran up to the counter and smiled. Mr. Matthews took his change, rang up the plane, and bagged it. Randall thanked Mr. Matthews, grabbed the bag, and ran out the door.

By this time, Sammy had a basket full of little things. She had discovered the bins of items that were five for a dollar. Her collection included barrettes, whistles, balls, a small coloring book, a few dolls that were one inch high, and one of those puzzles that had little squares you push around. "Can I get this for Christmas?" she asked Mama.

Mama and I tallied up all the items. It was more than five dollars. She was about to remove a few things when I said, "Don't. I got this."

"You don't have to use your own money."

"It's 'our' money and I'd like to. Besides, all this stuff will give us something for Sammy and me to do when we get back."

In the end, I only spent three dollars from the money Mr. Tash gave me. Mr. Matthews also didn't make me pay the quarter for Randall. What a fine day it turned out to be!

Sammy bounced in happiness until she froze at the edge of town and yelled, "Look!"

Leaning against our trailer door was a small, lopsided Christmas tree. Next to it sat a cardboard box and a rusty tree stand.

I pulled an envelope off the tree and handed it to Mama.

"Open it," she said.

I opened the envelope and pulled out a piece of paper that had "Sal's Pizza" stamped on the top. I softly read the words that flowed on the page.

Dear Tara, Sophie, and Sammy,

When you entered the pizza shop tonight it was like opening a Christmas present. It was so good to see you finally enjoying Christmas, or as Sammy said, "Having fun for Christmas." I told Sheriff Reynolds how I wish we could do something for you. He told me that you didn't have a tree. Together, Sheriff Reynolds, Sal and I decided to get you one. We called Mickey at the tree lot to see if he had any left. He said he had only one but wasn't selling it because it was too small. I told him it was perfect and I'd come by to get it, but since he was shutting down the lot for the night he said he'd

I waited silently to see Mama's reaction. She didn't like charity and this screamed charity to me.

Mama's shoulders relaxed. She took the letter from me, glanced at it, and then carefully folded it and tucked it back into the envelope.

"Do we have to take it back?" I asked.

"No, Sophie. I think we are done being grinches. What do you say? Shall we take this wonderful surprise into the house and set it up?"

Sammy and I both yelled, "Yeah!" The three of us tugged the tiny tree into the trailer. Mama called Sal's and spoke briefly into the phone. Before she hung up I heard her say, "Not this Sunday, I have to work, but we will see you on Christmas Eve."

We pushed the couch over to make room for the tree. Mama dampened a few cloths and we set about wiping down the really dusty ornaments. They were so beautiful. I was afraid Mama would tell us not to touch them. We didn't have any hangers, so Mama got some yarn from her bag and we used that to tie the balls to the branches. We found a shiny gold star and fixed it to the top of the tree.

We spent the next few days making paper garlands and homemade ornaments from a dough Mama made. When we were done, it was the most beautiful tree I had ever seen.

We always went to the cemetery on Christmas day, but this year was different. We went on Christmas Eve morning. Mama didn't cry. She smiled and placed a homemade ornament on the gravestone. She said a silent prayer, then said out loud, "I bet you put Betty up to getting that tree for us. I miss you, Bo."

I hugged her. "Mama, I'm glad you aren't frozen anymore."

It took Mama a second to realize what I meant. She had been as frozen as Granny Em and Grandpa Joe. She gave me a tight squeeze. "Me too, Sophie. Me too."

As we walked away I turned my head and whispered, "Thank you," to Daddy Bo.

At Church that night, I wasn't sure how they would react to our sudden appearance. After three years of not going, what would they say? What if they didn't want us there?

My fears, and all my doubts, about embracing Christmas went away amid the hugs and shouts of familiar voices.

They say that time heals all wounds

That's a bunch of crock

Hurt doesn't go away

It fades, but never disappears

But the cruel people die away

Memories get fuzzy

People need people

Kindness grows

In time

A new dynamic appears

Into which you can return into a community again

Mine for Eternity

Love Beyond Death

*F*rom the hotel parking lot, Rachel watched the neon sign. Blink, blink, blink. Green turned to pink, then back to green. Where the hell was he?

The October night approached the misty hours when even crickets fall asleep. Rachel shivered. She didn't bring a suitcase or a coat. Garret said she didn't need anything. He wanted to pick her up at her trailer after wrapping up the last shoot at the Haunted Mansion, but she didn't want her mom or any of her idiot friends to see her run away with him. So she walked the half mile to the motel down the road and waited.

Hollywood! Garret promised excitement. She could smell the freedom.

Her fists curled as she bounced up and down, her tight mini-skirt doing little to keep her warm. A small kernel of fear oozed into her consciousness. Rachel cursed. She wasn't used to waiting. Guys always picked her up on time even when she made them wait once they got there.

Then she remembered. The last time she made someone wait, they died.

A bald-headed man appeared from the shadows between the hotel office and the row of doors. Rachel's hands flew to her chest to stop her runaway heart. The man smiled, waved, and then disappeared into door number 2.

Before her heart could calm, headlights appeared on the two-lane highway.

"That better be him!" she muttered in a mixture of hope and anger. Her mind already forming the words to tell him off.

But the lights passed, and as they dimmed, so did Rachel's confidence.

"Shit!" The creep stood her up.

She glanced at the row of worn-out doors with numbers hanging askew, then looked into the dimly lit office where an old man slumped in a chair. She should go inside and see about getting a room. She had the two hundred dollars that she took from her mom's purse. A room in this dump certainly wouldn't be that much.

Another set of lights approached. Rachel lifted her eyes, her pupils growing smaller and then larger as the car passed. Her shoulders drooped but before she could step towards the office, one of the doors opened. Its number plate jiggled. A small shaft of light fell onto the cracked asphalt. A gnarly hand reached around the door and a man-shaped silhouette filled the frame.

Rachel ran to the office door and pulled. Her hands slipped off the locked knob. She jiggled it and then banged on the glass. "Hey asshole, wake up!"

She continued pounding the window but turned her head. The man, his face still in the shadows, walked toward her, confidently, like a cat approaching its prey. His hair turned green, then pink, then green.

She looked for something to break the window but didn't find anything. The man laughed. God, he was creepy.

She began to run away, onto the dark street, then stopped. She wasn't stupid. She wasn't about to run down a dark, lonely highway like those idiots who got into black cars with tinted windows or walked down dark stairs into basements. Damn, she shouldn't have watched all those clips from the horror movie Garret was making. She shook her head.

The man's feet scraped the pebbles on the sidewalk. Rachel spun around to face him.

"Get away, you..."

Words died on her lips at the sight of the oddly familiar face. It was covered in red scars as if someone rubbed a cheese grater over it. He reached for her with mangled hands.

NO! It can't be! Her voice trembled. "Johnny?"

The man's voice was deep and hoarse "What's wrong, Rachel? Don't like my new face?

Rachel relaxed her arms. "Garret, God, what an awful mask."

The man remained silent.

"Okay, Garret, you can stop pretending now, it's no longer funny."

"You're right, Rachel. Pretending isn't funny. But you like that, don't you? You pretended to love me, stringing me along. For an entire year, I did everything you asked of me. I cheated for you, stole the test answers, and even stole from my daddy for you. But I was just a big joke to you, wasn't I."

A maggot crawled out of Johnny's mouth and up his cheek. He grabbed it and threw it on the ground, never taking his eyes off of Rachel. "You know the worst of it? I saw you and your stupid friends drive by, laughing at me, but I pathetically waited by the neon sign thinking you'd come back on your own. Without them."

Rachel stepped backward holding her palm out to ward him off. Her hands shook. "Garret, stop."

"Oh Rachel, I'll stop. Just like my life stopped. I died waiting for my love."

Rachel rolled her eyes. "C'mon, Garret, it wasn't my fault the idiot Johnny waited until three a.m. and then got hit by that semi on the highway. Now stop this shit and let's get out of here."

A hand flew behind her neck and pulled her closer. The putrid smell hit her like a garbage truck.

"What are you doing, Garret? Stop it, right now." Rachel reached to pull the horrid mask off of Garret's head but it didn't come off. She saw maggots wiggling around rotten teeth.

"Surprise! It's not Garret, love. It's Johnny. I've returned from hell to claim my one and only love."

Rachel's frenzied attempts to pull away escalated the panic in her voice. "Stop it. I don't know who you are, but Garret will take care of the likes of you."

A deep-throated laugh escaped Johnny's feted mouth. "Poor Rachel. You really don't recognize me, do you?"

Johnny tilted his head. "Oh, I'm sorry, I forgot to tell you. Your hot-shot actor can't do anything now. You should have seen his car sink in the river. Glub glub glub, Garret dies in a tub."

Johnny pulled her closer.

Rachel closed her eyes, doubling her effort to pull free, but Johnny held fast.

"Do you know what, Rachel love? I had a choice. You know, at the pearly gates? I could have lived in paradise. But, the devil is, I couldn't go without you. I'm the luckiest guy in the world because now, you're mine for eternity.

Johnny ran his fingers through her hair then circled her throat. Rachel tried to scream but Johnny's squeezed harder. She couldn't find her voice. All that came out was a garbled squeak.

Rachel grabbed at his hands and put up a good fight. But the more she struggled, the stronger Johnny became.

"I love you, Rachel. Hell ain't so bad, you know. You'll fit right in. God, you are so beautiful and so…" Johnny licked his lips, "Perfect."

He stopped choking her long enough to hold her head between his hands. He leaned closer then covered her mouth with a kiss. His moldy tongue darted into Rachel's throat.

Rachel finally found her voice but it was too late. Her scream went straight to hell with Johnny.

Beware who you make fun of

They might come back

Dust Because

Love at First Sight

*D*usting sucks, but the two inches of dust on the windowsill wouldn't spontaneously combust itself away. Maybe my mom would. I don't mean blow up, or even dust the window, but perhaps she'd change her mind and not come next week. Then I wouldn't have to dust at all.

Getting my lazy ass in gear, I got up and headed to the kitchen to get the dusting supplies from under the sink. But when I entered the kitchen, I opened the refrigerator to get a drink and realized I didn't have any of Mom's wine. That wouldn't do. All I had was the cheap stuff in a box. Mom had to have wine from a proper bottle.

I grabbed the keys to old Betty, my '63 Beetle, and headed to the liquor store. We needed whiskey as well as wine. After going on a shopping binge and getting Jack Daniels, three bottles of white, three reds, and a couple of cases of Michelob for David, my neighbor, who pretended to be my boyfriend whenever Mom visited, I threw it all in the passenger seat and headed home.

I made it as far as the freeway access road but quickly got mired in a traffic jam. Shit. I turned on the radio and found that an accident had stopped traffic in both directions for several miles. I groaned, inched my way to the left lane, then made a U-turn in an emergency vehicle-only lane.

Sighing with relief that no flashing lights chased me, I drove onto the back roads. It took longer this way, but at least I was moving. I'd probably get home faster than if I waited out the accident.

Three miles past the Otis Mills Dairy farm and just before the old covered bridge, a chicken crossed the road. Unfortunately, I didn't have time to ask it "Why?" because Betty went flying into the ditch and all the alcohol hit the dash and exploded.

A few minutes passed by before I could understand what had just happened. Fortunately, Betty's seatbelt worked and I, unlike my bottles, was not plastered all over the windshield. I put Betty in reverse, but she wouldn't budge. I turned off the engine and pulled the lever to release the seatbelt, but it was stuck. I pushed, I shoved, I screamed, I swore, but nothing would release it.

There was nothing more I could do but dial 911.

"911. Please state your name and describe your emergency?"

"My name's Bunny and I'm stuck in my seatbelt. I can't get out."

A moment of silence passed before the lady said, "I'm sorry, Bunny, did you say you were stuck in your seatbelt?"

"Yes."

"Then why don't you drive to a place where someone can help you."

"Because my seatbelt is in my car that is stuck in a ditch in the middle of nowhere."

A snort came through the phone before the lady's slow words. "Can you tell me a little more about where this nowhere is?"

"I'm on Barrister Road just before the covered bridge."

"Okay, Bunny, stay calm. I'll send someone right out."

"Thank you."

She hung up between the "Thank" and the "you," and I think I heard her laughing too.

Glancing over at the glass carnage next to me, I noticed that the bottom of a broken whiskey bottle still had a jigger's worth of alcohol in it. I stretched to reach it and, careful to find the dullest edge of the glass, downed the whiskey.

The burn calmed me. I had nothing better to do, so when I spied the beer cans between the gear shift and the cushion, I didn't think twice. I popped one open and started drinking.

I saw the flashing lights behind me and gulped down a second can before throwing it into the back seat. I couldn't turn my body around to see the police cruiser, but I watched in my rear-view mirror. Two people spoke to each other, then one of them spoke into the radio. The driver got out, disappeared for a minute, and reappeared at my window. She rapped the glass with her knuckles.

It took me a minute to find the crank arm and, for some reason, my hand kept slipping off it, but I finally got the window open.

"Hello."

"Hello, ma'am. May I have your license and registration please?"

"Wait a minute." My arms flailed in the air trying to reach the glove box, but I couldn't.

I turned back toward the officer and shrugged. "I'm stuck."

With a glistening eye and a tinge of suppressed laughter, the officer tried to keep from smiling. "What's your name?"

"Bunny."

"Okay, Bunny, I'm going to open the door and help you out of the restraints. I'll look at your information when we know you're okay."

She opened the door and leaned over me to fiddle with the latch. I inhaled the scent of magnolias that came with her.

"Mm…you smell good." Oh God, did I just say that?

She turned her head. Her lips were inches from mine. "We're going to have to cut you out. Stay calm and wait right here."

Was that a twinkle I saw in her eye? When she disappeared from view, I felt alone and suddenly bereft. All I could think about were those green eyes.

She returned with a knife. "Now hold still."

After she sliced through the belt, I fell forward. She caught me and settled me back into my seat, her green eyes landing inches from mine.

"Fank you." I slurred and then attempted to turn so I could get out of the car, but the world spun around.

"Don't move, Bunny. The ambulance is on the way."

Ambulance? I couldn't quite understand why I needed one.

Green Eyes pointed to the broken bottles. "Have you been drinking?"

I couldn't remember. But I remembered the chicken, so I said, "Chicken."

Again, a hint of a smile crossed her lips and quickly disappeared. "Bunny, the ambulance just pulled up. We're taking you to the hospital. I'll follow right behind you."

"Hospital?" Why was my mind so fuzzy? "I got to dust."

Next thing I knew, I was in a white room surrounded by beeping things.

"Ah, you're awake. How are you feeling?" An officer got up from a chair by the door and walked over.

"Green Eyes?"

"Excuse me?" Green Eyes, as I thought of her, was having trouble hiding her smile.

"Nothing." I felt my forehead the way Mom used to when I was sick and cringed at the large bandage that I touched. "Fine, I guess I am fine."

"I need to take your statement. Can you tell me what happened?"

I thought for a moment, my brain still a little fuzzy. "Yeah. I needed to dust and..."

"I'm sorry, Bunny, did you say dust?"

"Yes. Dust."

Green Eyes shook her head. "Okay, continue."

"Like I said, I needed to dust, but I couldn't dust because we didn't have wine in a bottle."

Green Eyes cocked her head but didn't interrupt.

"Then I drove to get the wine and got other stuff I needed." I paused, out of breath, and seriously distracted by her beautiful face as she wrote something in a notebook.

Staring at her profile, I watched her long eyelashes flutter and her dimple dance as she wrote. She finished writing and turned those deep-green eyes toward me. She made one of those "keep going" gestures with her hand.

"The freeway was stuck." I closed my eyes and put my hand on my head, then winced from the contact with the bandage. "What did I just say?"

She shifted to her other foot but didn't say anything.

I added quickly. "Right. I didn't mean to say stuck, I meant jammed. The freeway was jammed. So, I took the back roads and this huge chicken came out of nowhere."

This time she interrupted. "A huge chicken? What was it doing?"

"Crossing the road."

"Indeed. Go on." Those dimples danced some more.

"Well, Betty didn't want to hit it, so she went into the ditch."

"Who's Betty? We didn't see another person. Do we need to look for her? Was she driving?"

It took me a minute to digest the barrage of questions, then I started laughing. "Sort of, ha ha ha ha. Betty's my car."

This time Green Eyes looked embarrassed. She cleared her throat. "I have to ask. Were you drinking while driving?"

"For goodness' sake, no. I had to dust, remember. I can't dust and drink. No, I was not drinking AND driving. I only drank after Betty went into the ditch. It was all I had left of my purchase." I sniffed and thought about the eighty dollars of booze that I lost. And poor Betty, she must smell terrible.

"Where is Betty?"

"She's…" She cleared her throat. "Your car was taken to Lou's Garage on South Street."

"Poor Betty. I guess that'll do. At least it's close to home. How bad is she hurt?"

"You'll have to call the garage for that."

I tried to sit up but then felt woozy.

She put her hand on my shoulder. "Easy, now. You hit your head quite hard."

"But I was stuck in the seat belt, how could I have hit my head?"

Green Eyes looked sheepish. "Well, my partner and I have a few theories about that. The first is that you weren't wearing it when you went into the ditch and then you put it on after so you wouldn't get a ticket."

"Safety first, always."

"Okay. Then here's our second theory. You know how when you get into a car you can pull the belt out to secure it, then it falls snugly back into place? We think your car's belt wasn't properly in place until you went into the ditch and then it ratcheted itself back the way it was supposed to. It would explain, then, why it was too tight on you. As for why the latch stopped working? I think we can say, your car…"

"Betty," I reminded her.

"Okay, Betty is pretty old."

I groaned.

"Look." Green Eyes lowered the notebook. "Do you have anyone who can take you home when they release you from here?"

"No, my mom's going to visit next week, but she lives twelve hours away."

Green Eyes reached into her pocket and handed me a card. "Here's my number. When they release you, call me and we'll escort you to your home."

Maybe I had drugs in my system, but that sounded like a proposition the way she said it. I shook my head clear. "Thanks." But I knew I wouldn't call. She was just being nice. Cute women like her never were interested in plain old me.

They kept me overnight for observation, then I took an Uber home the next morning. Thankful that it was Saturday and I wouldn't have to log on to work, I called my mom and told her what had happened, reassuring her that I was okay, and that she didn't need to rearrange her flight to come any earlier.

I hung up and found myself staring sadly at the dust on the windowsill. Damn, it hadn't been burnt away by the sun yet.

On my way to the kitchen to get the dusting supplies, my phone rang. "Bunny?"

"Yes?"

"This is George, from Lou's Garage."

"Oh, how's Betty?"

"Who's Betty?"

I laughed, "My car. It's the Beetle that was brought in the other day by the cops."

"Oh, that's what I'm calling about. I need to get your permission to continue with the repairs. It's going to cost 1,500 dollars and I need for you to sign an authorization for us to proceed."

I gulped. Betty was given to me by my grandmother, but damn if she wasn't costing me more than a new, used car would have. "I'll be there in about thirty minutes."

I walked back into the living room, gave the dust a quick stare, grabbed my keys, and then took off. Lou's garage was only a few blocks from my house, so I decided to walk to the garage and back. On the return trip, I stopped in the grocery store and picked up a bottle of wine, for me, not for Mom. I certainly needed it.

As I turned the corner on Barrister Road, a loud horn sounded. I heard a clucking noise and the next thing I knew, someone was shining a flashlight into my eyes.

When the light moved away, I couldn't believe who I saw. "Green Eyes?" I tried to get up. Pain shot through my ankle.

"Don't move, Bunny. We need to wait for the paramedics." Green Eyes smiled and pointed to the broken bottle of wine. "I see you lost another one." Then she laughed.

"What happened?"

A woman's voice rang from behind Green Eyes. "Oh, thank God you're alive. I am so sorry. If it weren't for that chicken, this never would have happened."

I couldn't believe it. I tried to move to see her face, but Green Eyes gently held me down. "Was it a huge red-winged chicken?"

"Yes! Thank God. You saw it too?"

Before I could answer, the ambulance pulled up and the paramedics took over. They wanted to take me to the ER to get an x-ray of my ankle. "It could be broken."

I tried to move my toes, but couldn't. "Damn! Ow!"

I looked at the EMT guys. "Do I have to go?" I didn't want to go there again. I wasn't sure my wallet would hold up to the pressure.

Simultaneously, they said no, but Green Eyes and the lady yelled, "Yes!" Then the lady added, "My insurance will pay for everything."

With that worry off my plate, I decided to take another trip to the ER.

Good thing, too. My ankle was broken and my knee was sprained. Her car hit me and it knocked me into the ditch. Later I found bruising all over my body, but at the time, I didn't feel anything but my ankle.

They put me under to set my ankle bones because the doctor had to put pins in it. When I woke, my room was filled with flowers in all shapes, colors, and sizes.

But they all paled in comparison to the vision that greeted me. She wore jeans and a T-shirt instead of a uniform and she still smelled like magnolias.

"Hi, Bunny." She smiled.

"Green Eyes?"

"You know you could call me by my real name."

I felt the blush coming on. "Um…what is it?"

"You really were out of it then. My name is Cassandra."

"Why are you here?"

"Because last time you woke, you didn't call me. I didn't want you taking an Uber again."

"Oh…" My mind went blank.

Cassandra smiled. It was like the sun rising in the morning. "Look, they won't let you go until after lunch. I'm going to run to the store and get a few things, then I'll swing back by and pick you up."

I still couldn't think of what to say, so I said the first thing that came to my mind. "Did you do all this?" I waved at all the flowers, a hopeful note in my voice.

"Oh, no. That was Mrs. Engle. She's the one who knocked you into the ditch. She'll come by before you leave to talk to you. She also left you a case of wine since she broke your bottle as well. It's in my car since the nurses wouldn't let her bring it in. I think it was too tempting."

Cassandra laughed, then continued talking. "I did bring you some flowers. It's the carnations in that teeny, tiny little vase over there." She pointed to a rolling table at the side of my bed.

My eyes turned back to hers. "They're beautiful!" I wasn't just talking about flowers.

A sound at the door announced the doctor and nurse's arrival. Cassandra waved to me and mouthed, "I'll be back. Don't go anywhere until I get here."

I watched her go. The lonely feeling returned.

True to her word, Cassandra returned and drove me home. She insisted on helping me into the house, then proceeded to make a "comfort" station next to the couch where I sat. Besides water in a new metal mug, a few bags of chips, an apple, and my bottle of pain medication, there was the latest best-seller by Ally Allowinter. "You got me a book."

"I hope you like it. She's my favorite author."

"Mine too."

It shouldn't have been awkward, but Cassandra stared at me and said nothing.

I fidgeted until I couldn't take the silence anymore. "Is something wrong?"

She cleared her throat. "Bunny, I like you. I don't know what it is, but there's something about you. Maybe it's the way you said chicken when you were in the car and talked about dust or something, but you made me laugh. I haven't laughed in a long time. So…" She paused and inhaled. "If you are straight, tell me now and I'll go. I never picked up the gay radar gene, so I have to ask."

Before I could answer, my neighbor David walked into the living room. "Bunny, I have a favor to…" His voice stopped when he saw my foot in a cast. He ran up to give me a gentle hug. "What happened?"

From behind David, I watched Cassandra's face fall. She quietly picked up her purse. "Cassandra, wait."

She turned and I saw the hurt in her eyes. Though it was sad to see, I couldn't help feeling giddy that she liked me. "David's my neighbor! He has a husband."

After the pain melted away, Cassandra extended her hand. "Hi, David. I'm Cassandra."

David looked from Cassandra to me then back to Cassandra as he pumped her hand with both of his. "It's nice to meet you. Really nice to meet you." He turned back to me. "Do you need anything? I'm heading to the store."

"No, thank you. Cassandra seems to have gotten everything."

"Alright then, I'll take off. Call me!"

After he left, Cassandra took a seat on the chair opposite me. She held out her hand. "Let's start again, this time without chickens, dust, and broken bottles. Hi, I'm Cassandra."

I put my hand in hers and felt warmth in my heart. "Hi, Cassandra. It's so wonderful to meet you." I laughed. "And yes, let's leave the chickens and the broken bottles, but I think…" I nodded toward the dust on the windowsill, "The dust may still be a problem."

An Unopened Letter

A Token of Love

Carolyn carefully held the small brown envelope addressed in beautiful calligraphy and wondered if she should open it. It was addressed to her late mother.

Miss Maggie McDonald,
AGIS, Montevallo, Alabama

The faded pink two-cent stamp never saw a post office. No ink proclaimed the day of delivery. Carolyn couldn't tell if the stamp had peeled halfway off from dried-up glue or years of fingers picking at its edges.

The letter came from Katie McDonald, who gave it to Maggie, Carolyn's mother, on the day Maggie left for college at Montevallo Girls' Technical Institute. Along with the sealed letter, Katie included a poem about the contents of the letter.

Inside the folds of paper, with its seams that are unbroken,
Are written words of wisdom, of hope that is unspoken
For when you fail and when you fall, for aren't we all mischievous
For when you feel that life's unfair and devils drive you devious
Look upon this missive as a seed of hope imparted
As a ray of sun to light your way in seas that are uncharted
When river despair runs through your mind and all your hope is gone
Tear open dear heart, these words of mine, and you will carry on.

Maggie kept the letter and poem, bundled together with a ribbon, in a wooden box. Before she died, Maggie gave the box to Carolyn. She told her that there was hope inside the letter and if she ever felt despair overwhelm her, she should open the letter and read the words inside.

"What's it say?"

"I don't know." Maggie shrugged.

"You mean you've never opened it?"

"No, I didn't. There were a few times when I held it and felt your grandmother's arms enfold me and heard her words. 'Maggie, there's always hope when you put your trust in the Lord, but if you feel lost, and the lord seems too far away, then open this.' She was right. I put my trust in

God and something always came along and relived my despair before I could rip open the envelope."

Maggie carried the envelope of hope through the birth of Carolyn and her brother Robert, two world wars, and eight grandchildren, not once opening it.

In her honor, Carolyn vowed to do the same. She put it on her dresser.

Like many trinkets, it became hidden under life. It sat ignored on Carolyn's dresser for another twenty years, a pretty box, a memento from her mother. It sat ignored through her own marriage, the birth of three children and her first grandchild, a divorce, and her battle with cancer, which is why she was being forced into an assisted living facility.

She didn't want to go. People died in those places. She didn't want to die.

Her children told her to collect what she wanted to keep. As she sifted through items on her dresser she found the box.

She opened the box, opened the bundle, and read the poem.

Carolyn imagined what words a mother might say to her child as she left to make her own way in the world. Good luck! Call me when you can. Let me know what you need and I'll try to get it for you. Watch out for boys! Save your money!

Or did the letter contain inspirational quotes or Bible verses? Perhaps Katie wrote stories of her own trials and how she overcame them. How much history might this letter contain?

Did Katie McDonald write "I love you" to Maggie?

Over and over, Carolyn read the last two lines of the poem while she considered the letter.

When river despair runs through your mind and all your hope is gone
Tear open dear heart, these words of mine, and you will carry on.

Carolyn felt despair. She knew the cancer would take her down. She knew that once she left her home, it would all be downhill. "Oh God, please, help me face what I need to face?" Fear gripped her. "I'm scared!"

Carolyn clutched her chest and felt the gold cross. She pulled the chain off her head. It was a necklace her mother had given her at her baptism. She forgot that she had thrown it on earlier.

Was this his answer? She trusted Him. Maybe He was telling her that she shouldn't despair.

She clutched both the cross and the letter to her heart as tears filled her eyes. No, she didn't need to open the letter. Hope still existed in Him.

After some time, she gently folded the poem and placed it on top of the sealed envelope. She searched around the house for a new ribbon, then tied up the bundle. Carefully, she put the bundle back into the box, laying the cross on top of it.

She pulled out her phone and called her granddaughter.

Kaitlin answered, "Grandma. Are you packed yet?"

"Almost. Can we stop for lunch before we go to the manor? I have something I want to give you before you head out to college."

"Okay, Grandma."

A memento is a time capsule of memories

Whether they are your personal experiences

or the stories shared by family and friends

they have relevance to your life

Hold on to them

(Unless they take up the entire house, then call a therapist.)

Pete the Scrappy

Love for a Pet

*W*hy did that dog keep following me? I must have some invisible sign that stray animals can read that says, "Look, here's a sucker! She'll help you."

The problem is, the sign is true. I am a sucker for strays. But it's harder in New York City than it was in Ithaca, mostly because of Mom. Whatever creature I brought home, she found a place for it until we could find it a new home or, as in the case of my last dog, until it grew old with us. I wished she could have found a place for my ex-boyfriend, but that didn't happen, which is why I moved to NYC in the first place.

New York is friendly to animal owners who can afford it. I can't, not to mention that my apartment's no-pet policy is non-negotiable. I've tried. I used to take the strays into my apartment to figure out where they should go, but somehow, I guess because of the barking and whining, the management found out, even though I fostered them for maybe three days, one week tops. At least the owners gave me a choice. Get rid of the dog and pay three hundred dollars or leave with the dog and forfeit my deposit.

The scrappy brown dog sure was cute, though. "Look, fellow. I can't take you right now. I have two interviews with possible clients and then I have to do a wedding. I don't have time and I can't afford you. Go find someone else."

The dog tilted his head. His tail wagged faster. He inched closer.

I felt the pull. My foot itched to take a step forward. I curled my fingers to keep from reaching out.

The dog tilted its head the other way causing its floppy ears to wiggle. I moaned. "Oh no you don't! I know what you're trying to do. Be all cute and all. Nope, it won't work. I'll see you later."

I escaped as fast as I could into the coffee shop. I picked up my cafe mocha and found a seat in the corner facing the door so I could see my potential clients when they arrived. I waited only five minutes but when the couple opened the door, I spied the dog sitting where I left it. I covered my eyes and shook my head.

"Hello, are you Bella?"

"Sorry, yes I am, please have a seat. Can I buy you a coffee?"

A little under two hours later, with two engagement sessions booked, I packed up my laptop and headed home to change for the uptown wedding that I was shooting tonight. I didn't see the scrappy dog when I exited the cafe and I wasn't sure if I felt sad or glad.

Walking in New York, even with hundreds of people around you, was like walking alone. Most New Yorkers didn't even see each other. I used to walk around saying hello to everyone, but after two years in the city, I became one of them. A silent cog in the wheel of commerce that spins on infinitely. I hated being a cog.

Tonight, however, the walk home felt different. I didn't feel invisible. Someone was watching me. I could feel it. After one block of feeling a little creepy, I turned suddenly, trying to catch the person following me. But nothing was there. I mean, there were lots of people, but nobody was paying attention to anything.

But the third time, I caught him. His little tail stuck out from behind a dumpster, wagging as if waving a flag of surrender.

"Are you following me?"

The dog slowly revealed himself and wagged his tail in overdrive to make sure I knew that he had decided I was the one.

"Look, you scrappy little bag of cuteness!" I sighed, "I don't have time tonight, but I can get you some food and leave it on the stairs of my apartment building for you. Follow me." I wasn't going to bring him inside, nope, I was not, but I'd feed him and maybe, if he was still around, take him to the shelter in the morning.

The dog recognized the win. He barked, ran up to me, and circled my legs. He must have had some training, because he didn't jump on me. "Good dog, now follow along."

I reached my brownstone. I looked down at the dog. "I have to get dressed and gather my gear. I have a job tonight. Why don't you go home, now?"

I felt terrible leaving him at the bottom of the steps, but what could I do? I could not afford him. I showered, dressed, ate a snack, and then peeked out the window. I didn't see him and felt sad but glad that he had moved on. But then I heard his bark.

I felt the zing of "Yeah, he hasn't left me!" right before I reminded myself, "Bella, no!"

But the poor thing had nothing to eat, so I put together a paper plate of ham slices, meatballs, and some leftover pasta. "This ought to do it."

The dog barked when he saw me as if saying, "I knew you would remember me!"

I put the paper plate down on the step. "Here you go! Now remember, after you eat, you have to go away." My taxi arrived and I waved goodbye to the dog.

The wedding I shot took two hours longer than it should have. Sometimes I think brides have no idea what they are asking for. "Take this additional picture, take that extra picture, it's digital so it shouldn't matter, right?" They have no idea how much time goes into processing afterward.

I dragged myself out of the Uber and onto the brownstone's stairs.

"Hey lady, give me your bags."

Oh shit, not again. I turned to the man who had come up behind me, then I looked for the Uber. Funny, my first thought wasn't, "Oh no, I'm being robbed." It was, "I'll never use that driver again. He didn't wait."

"C'mon lady, I don't have all night."

As a seasoned New Yorker, I knew that giving him what he wanted was the best thing to do for my safety, but I didn't want to lose my camera gear. And that bridezilla would haunt me for life.

The thief saw my hesitation. He pulled back to strike and I cringed. But then a ferocious bark announced the dog's entrance into our conversation. He shot out from the shadows. For a scrappy little dog, he packed a huge punch. The thief lost his balance and fell. The dog ran circles around him, paused for a moment to look at me, then kept running circles.

"Dog, I don't know why you are still here, but thank you." I ran up the stairs, opened the door, and scooted inside. Right before the door closed, I stopped it. That dog just saved me. "C'mon, doggie. Come on in."

As if he had been waiting for the invitation, he gave the man a chomp on the wrist, ran over his belly, up the stairs, and through the door.

The door latch clicked loudly in the foyer. We both breathed heavily. I stared at him and he stared at me. He parked his little butt on the carpet and aimed his cute, shining eyes at me saying, "Thanks, now what?"

My eyes stared back while I silently told myself, "Don't do it. Don't!"

I gave in first. "Well little guy, I think you just earned a night in a posh hotel." I scrunched my nose at the lie. "Okay, it's not posh, but it's better than the streets. Follow me."

We walked up two flights to my apartment. When I opened the door, the dog walked inside as if he knew he had to behave. He did a slow circle, then sat in front of the TV.

"So, you like watching TV? So do I, but I only do it when I'm done processing photos. Otherwise, I'd never get anything done. But not tonight. It's late, I'm tired, and frankly, that man put a real bee in my bonnet. Why am I staying in New York? I could be doing this same thing anywhere."

I walked to the closet and pulled out an old blanket, fluffed it, then put it on the floor. "Here you go. You can stay here tonight. Let me get you some water."

When I turned around with the bowl full of water, I noticed the dog furiously scratching. "Oh no! Do you have fleas?" I put the dish down. "You could use a bath!"

As if he understood the word "bath," the dog froze but the minute I picked him up he tucked his nose into my chest. The hug felt so good, I hugged him back, fleas and all.

In the bathroom, the dog tucked his tail between his legs as I ran the water. But the good dog that he seemed to be let me do what I needed to.

I didn't have any dog shampoo but figured the baby shampoo should do the job. He didn't argue or try to run away. It wasn't until the rinse water ran clear, after two applications of soap, that I deemed he passed the clean test. I unplugged the drain and when most of the water was out, and after the dog shook at least three times, I draped him in a towel and rubbed.

I watched in amusement as his back leg started tapping the floor. He rolled his eyes and pressed his head against my hands.

I knew then that I was a goner. Scrappy turned snugly as I rolled him onto his back and examined his belly. He had no ticks, but I managed to chase a few fleas around before picking them off. He stared adoringly at me for the entire process. "You're kind of cute and sweet! But you know that already, don't you?"

Satisfied that no more live critters lived on his skin, I carried him back to the living room and gently laid him on the blanket.

I almost thought of a name but stopped myself. If I named him, it would be harder. I gave him another pat on the head. "Goodnight, dog."

Though I didn't say them out loud, my brain scrolled through the list of possible names until I fell fast asleep.

I felt something on my chest. It weighed down on me. My eyes popped open ready to push off the intruder.

I swear the dog laughed the only way dogs know how to laugh. He barked, wagged his tail, and did a downward dog on my belly.

"Get off of me, you scrappy dog!" I pulled the covers over my head. "It's not time to wake up."

The dog barked again with a "Please, I gotta go."

I wish Mom were here, I could sleep in, but I knew that wouldn't happen now. The dog needed to go.

"Fine." I grabbed my robe and slippers and walked the dog down the stairs to the front door, glad he hadn't decided to lift his leg on the fake potted plants.

He darted to the bushes as soon as I opened the door. As I watched, a niggling beast on one side of my brain said, "Shut the door. Don't let him back in." But the other side, the bigger, stronger dragon slayer, that killed its foes with no thought to the possible repercussions, won out.

As if sensing my inner turmoil, the dog walked slowly to the door and sat on the top step, tilted his head, and proceeded to give me the "I'm just a cute little puppy who loves you and will do anything for you" look that always turned me into their slave.

"Well, what are you waiting for? Come back inside, boy."

After feeding him some more leftover meats, I called the local vet. Thankfully, they had a cancellation and would love to take a look at the stray dog and check for a chip.

I wrapped a bandanna around his neck as a makeshift collar. Dog, as I started calling him, didn't mind me carrying him for the two blocks to the vet office, but somehow, his, "Oh no, not in there!" vet-o-meter kicked in the minute we stood at the entrance door.

"Dog, quit fighting. They just want to see if you have a chip and check for bugs. Here." I darted inside the door and grabbed a dog treat from the bowl on the counter. "Chew on this."

Dog stopped wiggling and ate the treat. I grabbed a handful of the treats and continued feeding him until we were called into the tiny room.

The vet checked him out. "He doesn't have a chip and, except for a few patches of dry skin, he seems pretty healthy. I'd say he's about four years old." The vet rubbed behind his ears. "Hey, little guy. You're looking pretty good." She looked at me. "Shall we start a file for him under your name or are you taking him to the pound?"

The dog heard the word "pound" and locked eyes with me.

Did he understand what the vet just asked? "May I have a minute with him?"

"Sure, I have a patient in the other room. You have about twenty minutes before our next one is due in here."

I plopped down next to the dog on the floor and rubbed his head. "You know, it's like you knew I didn't want to be in NYC anymore. I've been toying with the idea of moving back to Ithaca for a while now. You know, getting out of this rat race. What do you say, want to come with me?"

The dog rolled onto his back asking for belly rubs.

"I guess that's a yes. First, though, I have to call Mom and make sure it's okay. Then we have to think of a name for you. I can't keep calling you Dog, now can I?"

I reached for my phone and pressed the number for Mom. She answered on the second ring.

"Hi, Mom!"

"Bella, how are you?"

"I'm doing okay. Look, I don't have a lot of time to talk, but can I come visit this weekend? I have a surprise for you."

"Sure, you know you can come anytime."

"Okay, I'll come on Friday." She hung up and I hugged the dog. "Looks like you and I will be friends for a long time. She's been begging me to come home since I left."

I picked up the dog and headed to the front desk. "How much do I owe you for today?"

The tech gave me a figure. "Shall we start a file on him?"

This question solidified my decision. I rubbed his furry head. "No, I think I will be moving back to Ithaca and I'll take him to a vet there. Can you just give me a copy of today's visit?"

"Certainly will." The tech fluffed the dog's ears. "Looks like you found a new home, little guy."

The lady gave me a leash and we walked the long way home, past the park.

As we got closer, he pulled on the leash. Curious as to what he thought was so exciting, I followed him.

He led us right to a hotdog truck. He sat and barked three times.

An older man turned around, laughed, and addressed the dog. "Pete, where've you been?" The man reached into a small container, pulled a hotdog, and threw it.

I watched the dog, Pete, I guess, swallow the thing in one gulp. I laughed. "So his name's Pete?"

"That's what I always called him. He's been stopping by my stand every morning when I open and every night when I shut down. I give him the hotdogs that were on the burner too long." The man picked out another hotdog and threw it to Pete.

I knelt to pet the dog. "Pete. That's a good name. Pete, the Scrappy."

The man looked my way and gestured to the hotdogs rotating on a burner. "I see that Pete's found a new friend. Do you want a dog? It's on the house. Any friend of Pete's is a friend of mine."

I agreed to a loaded hot dog. "What's your name, sir?"

"Sir, who's a sir, my name's Jim."

"Well, Jim, thank you for taking care of Pete."

"T'weren't nothing. He's a good dog. Keeps the rats away. But I guess I need to start feeding another stray, is that the case?"

"Yes, Pete's coming home with me."

The trip to Mom's house involved the usual traffic vying for first place out of New York City. Pete ran back and forth between the windows, barking in the back seat at the trucks and cars as they zoomed past me. I could almost hear him yelling, "Hey, idiot, it's a highway, not the motor speedway. Slow down!"

I couldn't agree with him more. I hated traffic.

Eventually, the barking stopped. I looked in the mirror and he had curled up by the window.

As the car pulled into my mom's driveway, Pete slowly woke.

"We're here, Pete." I got out, scooped him up, and turned to the house.

Mom ran out the door to greet us. When she saw Pete, she ran up to me and pulled him out of my hands. "What an adorable little guy!" She looked at me. "Is he yours?"

"Thanks for the hug, Mom."

Mom moved in and squeezed me. "Sorry, you know how I am with animals."

"I know, I'm just like you."

"Let's go inside and you can tell me all about the surprise you have for me."

Mom had brownies and milk on the table ready for me, but she walked straight to the fridge with Pete in her arms. "What'll it be, chicken or steak?"

"Mom, I have dog food in the car."

"That's okay, we can spoil him a little. Right, Pete?"

While I ate my brownies, Pete munched on leftover chicken. Mom asked, "So, what's my surprise? You can't keep your old mom waiting too long."

"How would you like me and Pete to move in?"

"For good?"'

"Yes, for good. Or until I marry, which may not be in your lifetime."

Mom waved her hands at the marriage comment, but I think the entire neighborhood heard her screams of delight paired with Pete's excited barking.

The unconditional love from a pet

Will never let you down.

My Dragon

Love of an Invisible Friend

*I*n an assisted living home, William stared at nothing. His blue eyes had stopped working months ago. The stories of his life, etched on his shrunken face, wrote a tale spanning ninety-six years.

He felt something land on his chest, gently, like someone placed a warm blanket near his neck or like a cat snuggling to get warm. The faint odor of pine needles brought back a memory from when he was five years old.

"Avalon, is that you?"

"Hello, William."

William tried to smile, but his muscles didn't want to move. He was so thirsty.

Reading his thoughts, Avalon reached over to the tray near the bed and dipped his talons into a glass of water, then rubbed them on William's lips.

The touch gave William enough strength to whisper. "I thought you were forever gone. That you had forgotten me?"

"I have never forgotten you and, like I promised, I am here to be with you when you need me the most."

His shallow breath made it hard to speak and his lips quivered. "But Avalon, I shunned you. I…" William inhaled deeply, his breath stopping for a few seconds, and then continued. "I stopped believing in you. I forgot about you."

Avalon tucked his head under the man's chin and hugged his old friend with his wings. He listened to William's heart beating ever more slowly. " My friend, you haven't forgotten, just moved me out of your life for a while, but I've always been in your heart. That's how I knew to come. You needed me and your heart remembered."

William tried to pick up his hand to pet Avalon, but to no avail. It shook but did not move. He groaned. "I want to touch you, to feel your silky smooth skin, to see you."

"Just relax, it will be okay. You'll see."

William heard Avalon's deep voice and calmed a little. "Please, Avalon, can we do it. Can you take me there again even though I'm blind?"

Avalon smiled, stood, and looked deep into William's unseeing eyes. He put a claw on each temple and their minds met.

William could see his friend, just like when he was a child. Avalon's blue and gray scales, like those of a lizard, were as smooth as glass. His tail still had that arrowhead at the end of it, and his head still looked like a mixture between a crocodile and a seahorse.

Avalon expanded his body, growing to the size of a small donkey. He extended his bat like wings and smiled. "Are you ready?"

William climbed on his back. They soared through the sky and flew into the clouds, then dove into the oceans sending schools of fish scattering in all directions. William whooped. "It is just like it used to be. Whoo hoo…"

Dr. Jill Worthington entered William's room. She noted the pale skin of his face and the shallow breathing. She checked his pulse, then called William's family. "He doesn't have much longer. Are you sure you won't come? "

Jill listened for a minute, then pocketed her phone. She picked up William's cold hand and sat next to him on the bed. "I am here, William." She watched his face quiver. His eyes started moving beneath his eyelids, then he smiled and his eyes popped open. She felt heat in his hands. For a minute, it seemed a miracle was to take place but then William frowned, closed his eyes, and drew his last breath.

Jill waited in the quiet. She hated this part of her job. Pronouncing the dead seemed so final. There had to be more, so she waited. Every time, she gave the deceased a few moments of peace before she called down to the morgue.

She was just about to get up to write on the clipboard when she saw him. She rubbed her eyes. How long had her shift gone on? She was so tired. She blinked, expecting him to disappear, but he was still there.

"Well, Jill, aren't you going to say hello?"

Avalon scooted away from William. His scales changed from blue to a deep, dark pink before he flew into Jill's lap. "Remember me? You did a lovely thing holding William's hand. He knew he wasn't alone when he left."

Jill tried to speak, but no words came.

"I have to go now." Avalon leaned in and gave Jill a kiss on her cheek. "It was good to see you. I will return when you need me the most." Avalon blew out a puff of smoke and disappeared.

Jill sat quietly until her breathing became normal and she found her voice. "ALLY?" She shook her head. She hadn't thought of her childhood friend, her pink dragon, in years. He was always there for her on those long, lonely days before her mother woke from a drunken sleep. She remembered all the beautiful emotions and feelings of flying through the air.

Sighing, she got up and wrote on William's chart. Time of death: 10:00 PM. Cause of death: Natural, old age. Notes: William died with two friends by his side.

My imaginary friends

You may not see them

You may not hear them

But that doesn't matter

Because they are mine

The Grown-Up Table

Love in Traditions

*G*rown-up food is scary looking. Why did I have to sit here this year? Oh yeah, I turned twelve five days ago. You'd think they'd wait at least a year. Don't I need to experience being twelve before they plop me down at the grown-up table? I tried to get out of it, but Mom said Grandmother would be disappointed. So here I was.

I stared at the plate of lettuce. A slimy light-brown sauce oozed off the pile onto the plate.

My grandparents sat stiffly at opposite ends of a really long table, nodding their heads in response to something my mom said. All the ladies at the table, my four aunts, my mom, and me, glittered with our festive red dresses. My dad and his brothers wore suits and ties. I pulled at the neck of my itchy dress and picked up a fork.

Aunt Beth, seated at my right, nudged me with her elbow. "Hey, that's the wrong one. Remember, start from the outside and work your way in."

"Sorry, thanks," I whispered back.

"No problem."

I longingly glanced at the den. Shrieks of laughter from my younger cousins wafted through the air. Sometimes it sucked being the oldest kid.

With pangs of hunger gnawing at my tummy, I tasted a small piece of lettuce. Fearing the worst, I held my breath, but then the sweet yet tangy taste filtered through. Yum. I filled my fork for the next bite. I opened my mouth wide to stuff it all in when Aunt Georgia, who sat across from me, kicked my feet under the table and mouthed, "Too much." She held up her fork with just three little pieces of lettuce on it, like one of those commercials demonstrating how something works, and slowly lifted it to her mouth. I counted nine pieces of lettuce crammed onto my fork and sighed. I shook the lettuce off my fork, which made the dressing splatter. I glanced up at Georgia thinking she'd scold me, but she rolled her eyes, making me choke on the goofy laughter that rose to my throat.

Aunt Beth tapped my back. "Are you okay?"

"Yes, Aunt Beth. I just swallowed too much at once."

I stabbed at the lettuce trying to get only three pieces onto the fork. It wasn't as easy as Aunt Georgia made it look. When I managed to collect two small wedges, I gave up and aimed them towards my mouth. I glanced at Aunt Georgia again, lifting my fork as if to say, "Like this?" She smiled and nodded.

Mom came over and reached for my plate. A pile of lettuce remained to be attacked by my fork, but she picked it up anyway. Before she walked away she touched my shoulder and leaned into my ear. "You're doing great. Keep listening to Georgia and Beth."

Candlelight sparkled off the many glass and silver bowls. A cup of red stuff sat in a dish on my red place mat. Curious, my spoon hovered over it but then Uncle Joe, who sat on my left, cleared his throat and shook his head.

It felt like forever before one of my mom's fancy dinner plates landed in front of me, the gold edges circling the tiniest piles of food. Where was the big pile of potatoes and the huge pile of turkey?

Instead, next to the single, lonely turkey slice, sat a small pile of mashed potatoes the size of a golf ball. The carrots, all three of them, rested side by side like a fallen picket fence. Grownups sure did eat weird.

My stomach growled again and my fingers itched to pick up a fork. But I listened to what Mom told me to do. "Whatever you do, don't speak unless asked a question, and don't eat unless someone else starts."

Once we all had a plate, the dainty eating began again. The hunger pangs made me grumpy. I whispered to Aunt Beth, "Is this all we get?"

"Yeah, that's it." She smiled then leaned over. "That's why we have the after-party. Once Grandmother and Grandfather go home, we'll dig into the leftovers. You get to join us now! But I think you're still too young for the wine."

"Oh, goody."

Boringness filled the air. They spoke on and on about market shares, stocks, and employee stuff. I tuned it all out. They were so busy talking I didn't think anybody would notice me. I picked up the slice of turkey and quickly pushed the entire thing into my greedy mouth. I almost groaned in happiness. It took a minute for my ears to notice the quiet and my blue eyes to see the twenty-two eyes staring at me. I swallowed, the huge wad of turkey scraping my throat as I forced it down. "What?"

Grandmother's mouth stretched in what looked like a smile. "Molly, how is your school going? Do you like the Academy?"

I carefully gulped some water from a crystal glass that I was afraid of breaking and then said, "Yes, Grandmother, thank you."

"I knew you would like it. All Worthingtons do well there."

Silence rose again. Was I supposed to say more? Thank God for Uncle Joe. The minute he said, "Remember that time when…" stories from days at the Academy flooded the table. All my relatives had gone to the Academy, and Grandmother made sure the rest of us would, too.

I returned to being invisible and I liked it better that way. Grandmother didn't speak to me any more that dinner.

Dessert time arrived. My body shook with excitement just waiting for it. I almost cried when it arrived. The playing card–sized slice of apple pie, crowned with a dot of whipped cream the size of a quarter, laughed at me saying, "It's the grown-up table, what did you expect?"

I wanted more pie, and where was the ice cream? At least there was only one fork left, so I didn't have to worry about using the wrong one.

I gobbled my pie in two bites. I glanced around. Everyone else's forks daintily picked up small pie pieces. It took them forever to eat one slice.

Finally, Mom said, "Molly, you may be excused."

I jumped up and my napkin fell onto the floor. Before I could run away, Aunt Beth stopped me with a hand on my shoulder and mouthed, "Pick up your napkin and say it properly."

I bent to pick up the napkin and made a big production of folding it and gently placing it on my plate. I walked to Mom and kissed her cheek. "Dinner was lovely, Mom. Thank you."

She leaned over and whispered in my ear. "You did great, honey, I'm so proud of you. Now say goodbye to your Grandmother and Grandfather."

I straightened my back, plastered on a smile, and approached the end of the table. Unsure of what to do, I made a bowing type gesture. "It was nice being with you. Please excuse me."

They put down their forks with the slightest "ting" on their plates, dabbed their lips with their napkins, then looked into my eyes. "You're a lovely young lady. Now run along. We'll see you next Thanksgiving."

I ran to the den and grabbed Billy's popcorn bowl.

"Hey, get your own."

He tried to pull it back, but I was bigger and stronger. Sometimes it paid being the oldest.

I squeezed onto the couch between Billy and my three other cousins, Josie, Brad, and Peter. "I'm so hungry!"

"Didn't you just eat?"

I shoved the popcorn into my mouth and mumbled, "Yeah, bud there wadn't a lotta food."

"Really?"

I swallowed. "Yeah. Don't be in a hurry to be a grown-up. They don't eat anything."

My five other cousins, ranging in age from two years old to nine years old, collectively yelled from the floor in front of me. "Be quiet!"

I grabbed another handful of popcorn, shoved it into my mouth, and settled in to watch the movie.

From eating popcorn with your fingers

To the salad fork and polite conversation

I wonder when a child transitions

Me, I'd rather eat popcorn

Bad Timing

Tragic Love

*H*e swooped in, looked her up and down, and whistled a low cat call. Then he turned to the bar. "I'll have what she's having."

Lucy almost choked on the last sip of her special soda.

Joe, the bartender, raised his eyebrows at Lucy and she shrugged. "Go ahead."

While waiting for the drink, the man introduced himself. "Hi, I'm Ryan and you are the most beautiful woman I've seen in ages."

Tilting her head, Lucy laughed. "Then you must have been sequestered somewhere for a long time."

Buck put the glass in front of Ryan, but his eyes met Lucy's posing a silent question. When Lucy shook her head, he added a glass of water to the counter and they both waited.

Ryan picked up the drink and took a large sip, then immediately spit it back into the glass and started gasping. "What's in this? Gasoline?"

She couldn't help laughing at him. "That's what you get for trying to pick up a poor, helpless woman."

He picked up the water and chugged it. Then he placed it tenderly on the bar and looked at her. "Really, what's in that?"

"It's mixture of Coke, tomato juice, and hot pepper sauce." She reached over and took a sip of Ryan's. "I think my brother Buck may have gone a little heavy on the pepper. He's just looking out for me."

"He's your brother?" Ryan looked at Buck. "Ah, I see it now, same brown hair, eyes, and nose." He turned back to Lucy, "But you're much prettier.

Buck slapped a bar towel at Ryan.

"Hey, why'd you do that?"

Lucy stood and grabbed Ryan's hand. "It means he likes you. C'mon, I'm hungry."

He followed her out mumbling, "That's a funny way to show it."

Once they were outside the bar, Lucy dropped his hand. "So, Ryan who doesn't like my special drink, I am hungry. Are you hungry?"

Ryan rubbed his bare arm where the towel left a red mark. "That depends. Do you have more brothers waiting with towels to beat me with?"

Lucy laughed, "No, it's just the best place ever. I love their steak burgers."

"You got me at burgers. Lead the way."

They walked three blocks to JJ's Diner, Lucy's favorite place to eat. It was cheap and they gave you tons of delicious food. They ordered and then talked.

Ryan took a sip of his water and asked, "So what's a beautiful woman like you doing all by yourself in a bar on a Friday night."

"I was hanging out with my family. My brother tends to the bar, my mom organizes the snacks, and my grandfather owns the place. "

"Wow, that's terrific. So do you work there too?"

"Hell no, I am an ER nurse, I take care of all the idiots that get too drunk and end up at the hospital. What do you do?"

Ryan glanced out of the diner window, then took another sip of his water. "I'm a private contractor in logistics."

"Sound's glamorous." Lucy fanned her face with her hands like she held a paper fan and blinked her eyes.

"Sometimes it can be quite interesting. Like the time we helped Ringling Brothers get to their next booking when their train derailed.

"Did you see lions and tigers and bears? "

And so their conversation went, each giving a little more about their lives and their past. After talking for three hours, Ryan suggested they walk to the water to watch the sun set. They continued sitting on a bench overlooking the water, occasionally throwing their leftovers at the seagulls. Sometimes, Ryan would stand up and start singing, then invite her to dance with him, right there by the water, in view of everyone that walked by. Then they'd sit and talk more. He made Lucy laugh and filled her with desire.

At midnight, they heard the bell at St. John's chime the hour. Lucy looked at her watch. "Oh my, I have to be at work in four hours."

"Let me call a cab."

Ryan accompanied her to her home in Manyunk, Pennsylvania, where she still lived with her parents. After telling the driver to wait for him, he walked her to her front door. There, he held her gently and kissed her. "Lucy, I've just met you, but I think I'm in love. Meet me at the Liberty Bell on Sunday at 3. I'll have a surprise for you." He turned without another word and left in the cab.

Lucy arrived at Independence Hall fifteen minutes early. After an hour, she doubted she had heard him right, so she walked a few blocks to the pier. He wasn't there either. She went back to the Liberty Bell. She spent the next two hours walking back and forth, wondering if she got the time or location wrong. Her feet ached from the high heels she wore and soon the cold that seeped into her thin jacket chased her back to the bar. She argued with herself as she walked the few blocks .

"Whad'ya expect? Ya met him in a bar for Chrissakes."

"You should have waited longer. Maybe something happened?"

For days after, she chastised herself for her foolish thoughts. But no amount of self-pity could erase the tingle of his gentle touch when he cupped her cheeks to kiss her. His kiss felt like his entire soul depended upon her response. And didn't he say he loved her?

She wished she'd taken a selfie with him, but she didn't pull out her phone the entire night. Their time together replayed in her head for months until she gave up trying to find him.

***

Perhaps the right man hadn't come yet, but Lucy found everyone after Ryan to be shallow, awkward, or just too bossy. She shuddered at some of the sloppy, wet kisses that she endured. In order to move on, she imagined that Ryan had died. It hurt to think that, but it hurt more to think he didn't want her after all.

Even Kenny, when she first met him, didn't pass muster, but he grew on her, like certain foods become your favorite after you've eaten them a time or two. He made her feel loved and protected, and their lovemaking was nice. It never reached the ideal that Lucy had imagined with Ryan, but most times, it was enough.

Six months into their relationship, and she couldn't shake the nagging in her brain. "Why are you still with him. He's not what you want?" But like a child with a favorite blanket, she stayed with him. When his company transferred him to Washington, DC, she decided to go with him.

Before they left, he blindsided her at the going-away party with a proposal. That sparkly diamond glared at her, daring her to break Kenny's heart.

She said yes.

Three weeks before the wedding, while waiting for her train, Lucy saw Ryan walk onto the platform. She blinked a few times. How tired was she that she was seeing ghosts?

She slowly stood and walked toward him. She had to be sure.

He looked as handsome as he did in the bar that night but he seemed less boy like. Dark circles under his eyes hinted at long, hard hours.

He was so lost in thought that he didn't see her.

"Ryan?"

He twisted around like a master in martial arts, recognized her, and then relaxed. "Lucy?"

Anger welled up in her hands and she slapped him.

The train came. Nobody got out and nobody got on. The train left.

Ryan rubbed his cheek. "I guess I deserved that." He gently touched Lucy's elbows. "How are you, Lucy?"

She shouldn't have felt it. She was engaged to Kenny. But the zing of his touch took her right back to those porch steps. She felt the need for more. The promise of unfulfilled passion overwhelmed her.

"Kiss me."

Ryan gently pushed her back from him. "What?"

She didn't wait. She leaned in and kissed him.

When their lips parted, Ryan's eyes reflected the passion that she felt. She took his hand and pulled at him. "C'mon, I'm hungry." "Wait, where are we going?" "I don't care, anywhere, as long as I don't have to think."

For one night she became someone else in his arms. Once they entered his room, they forgot all about ordering room service and made love. Sweet, passionate, better than her imagination kind of love. Ryan set her on a pedestal and catered to her every need. Afterward they ordered food and talked about the night they met. Stomachs full, they made love again.

As they lay in bed with the exhaustion one only gets from exposing their mind and body to endless pleasure, Ryan brought up the subject of his disappearance. "I'm sorry, Lucy."

She didn't have to ask him what he was talking about. "What happened?"

"My sister called to tell me that my mother was in the ER. They live in LA, so I took the first flight out there. I was going to see her, then call the bar to let you know I wouldn't make it, but on my way back to my mom's house, I got hit by a car. The coma lasted over three months. When I came out of it, I couldn't walk. After six months of rehab, I could finally support my own weight and walk. By that time, I figured you had moved on. I didn't try to contact you."

Lucy's heart wrenched and she snuggled into him. They fell asleep. In the early hours, Lucy got up to use the bathroom. She saw Ryan's wallet lying on the night table. She glanced at his beautiful sleeping body and realized that she still didn't know his full name. She picked it up to look at his ID. A photo of Ryan in a tux supported by crutches while he hugged a beautiful, pregnant woman wearing a bridal gown, fell to the floor. When she picked it up, she flipped it over and read, "Our wedding day." That's when it hit her.

She knew nothing of him. Could that be his wife? The pain hit like a snake bite. With shaking hands, she shoved the photo back into the wallet and tossed it, as if it would burn her, back where she found it.

What had she just done?

She dressed hurriedly and left him sleeping on the bed.

The "Ch-chunk, ch-chunk" noise of the subway car matched the tennis match in her brain. "Do I tell Kenny?" "Should I pretend it never happened?" "Kenny will know." "He'll never find out." "It's not fair to Kenny." "What am I doing?"

She didn't worry about the fact that she hadn't come home and hadn't spoken to him. She often volunteered for extra shifts without calling him because she didn't want to wake him. But she knew that she'd never be able to face Kenny without guilt. Maybe this thing with Ryan was her wake-up call.

Kenny knew something was wrong the minute she walked through the door.

"Lucy, are you okay? Did something happen at the hospital?"

The tears ran quickly. Lucy gulped a few times before talking.

"I'm so sorry, Kenny." I couldn't look him in the eye. "I feel awful. I've been lying to you. I don't love you, I've loved someone else for a while, and last night I…" She couldn't say it.

Kenny, after a long pause and with ever loving patience, hugged her. "It's okay, Lucy. We can work it out." Lucy was about to respond but he held up his hand. "I know you don't love me as much as I love you, but we are good together. Sometimes that's all we can ask for."

He pulled away and looked into her teary eyes. "Please give us a chance?"

She couldn't look at his pleading face. How could he still love her after she told him that. He deserved better. She shook her head and tried to pull away.

"Don't, Lucy. Don't pull away. I love you."

Lucy looked at him then. She noticed his tears.

Kenny rubbed his hands on her shoulders, an affectionate gesture that used to comfort her but now felt like razors on her burning arms. "Look, I have to go to work and you look tired. Why don't you go to bed and we can talk about this when I get back. Please say you won't leave while I'm gone."

Not knowing what else to say, she just nodded. He let her go when she pulled away this time, and she went into the bedroom and closed the door.

He left for work about thirty minutes later. After she heard the door click, Lucy found her suitcase and started packing. That's when she realized that she never fully committed herself. She had gone from living with her parents to living with Kenny. Except for her clothes, her laptop, and a few trinkets she got as gifts, everything belonged to Kenny. She didn't write a note but before she closed the door on Kenny forever, she whispered, "I'm so sorry. I hope you find the woman who deserves you."

The Uber took her to a hotel room across town where she spent several hours agonizing over what to do before falling into a fitful sleep. She had to get away. Away from all of them with their many expectations. And then it hit her. Her whole life she'd been living to fit into what other people thought she should be. Well, that was going to change. No more would her family or her boyfriend or that lying, cheating Ryan ever dictate what she would do.

She called the hospital and informed them that she would be quitting and would use up her leave time before her termination date. Kenny, her mom, and Buck called her cell several times, but she let all the calls go to voicemail. She needed to get a new phone, too.

When she couldn't make up her mind about where to go, she opened a map of the United States on her laptop, closed her eyes, and pointed. When she opened them, her finger was on a little town named Bandera, Texas, near San Antonio.

After applying for a job at a local hospital there, she found a hotel and made reservations. Then she called her mom.

"Hi, Mom."

"Lucy, are you okay? Where are you?"

"Before I say anything, can you get Dad and put me on speaker phone?"

"Sure, honey. Wait a second." She heard her dad shuffle into the room. "Okay, go ahead."

"Mom, Dad, I'm not getting married and I'm moving. I'll let you know when I'm settled."

Her mom and dad exploded with questions. Lucy pulled the phone away from her ear until they stopped yelling. When the volcano of emotions stopped, Lucy felt the tug of comfort. They loved her and would do anything for her. But she had to look out for herself even if she wasn't sure what "herself" looked like. She had to find out.

"I'm not coming home and I'm not going to let you know where I am until I'm settled. But I will keep in touch so you won't worry. And if Kenny calls, please tell him I'm sorry."

She hung up the phone before they could convince her to change her mind.

***

Adjusting to the slower pace of the Bandera emergency room took a while and left Lucy with too much time to think about Ryan. Why couldn't she let go? It wasn't like they spent much time together.

To keep her brain occupied with other things, she volunteered for extra shifts until one day, her coworker Ramona took her aside, handed her a cup of coffee, and said, "You need a hobby other than work. Do you ride?"

Under the watchful eye of Ramona's husband Tyler, Lucy became an adept horsewoman and made two new friends. After Ramona tried to set her up on a few blind dates, everyone learned that Lucy put men in the "friends only" category.

She enjoyed riding and one day, after a long ride, Ramona made a joke. "If you don't want a man, maybe you should get a horse."

Lucy finished turning out the horse she rode that day, then asked Ramona, "Do you think Tyler would let me board one here?"

Ramona smiled. "Another horse? I know Tyler wouldn't say no to that."

And so Lucy found herself the proud owner of a four-year-old Paint mare that she named Frisky because the horse stole things from her back pockets.

Riding and owning a horse led Lucy on a path of discovery about herself and what she wanted out of life. She did things that made her happy and she didn't worry about pleasing other people. She found that caring for Frisky gave her peace, especially in the early mornings when the sun peaked over the horizon. A desire to own her own place, where Frisky could be in her backyard, became too strong to resist.

She spent the next three years saving up enough money to buy a small property near Ramona and Tyler's ranch. It came with a paddock and a barn. Friday night dinners at Ramona's became routine. Though Ramona and Tyler still invited other people, sometimes single men, to these dinners, Lucy no longer worried about being set up. Everyone enjoyed the good food with no expectations.

Soon after Lucy moved into her new home, Ramona knocked on her door after she returned from her hospital shift. When Lucy answered it, Ramona smiled and said, "You need a man!"

"What?"

"I said, you need a man and I have just the one for you."

"Now wait here, Ramona, I stopped worrying about you bringing single men to Friday dinners because they're your friends and you've always invited people over, but I'm not going out on a blind date with anyone. You agreed."

"I know I did and I ain't going back on my word. You know I'm your friend, right?"

Hesitantly, Lucy huffed, "Yes."

"Okay then. Close your eyes and wait. I'll be right back. Don't peek.

Just wait here and I'll introduce you."

Lucy heard the car door slam and then Ramona whispered. "Sh, sh, sh. It's okay. C'mon, meet the lady of the house. When she opened her eyes, ready to yell at Ramona, Lucy's heart melted.

Ramona held out the Labrador puppy and laughed. "Lucy, meet your new man. He doesn't have a name yet, I'll leave that up to you."

Lucy grabbed him out of Ramona's arms and hugged him. "He's so adorable! And so soft. He's perfect. Thank you, Ramona."

"He's the runt of the litter and Tyler figured it would be good for you to have him. I agreed. Are you still coming to dinner on Friday? If so, bring him along."

She started walking away, then turned back. "Oh, I almost forgot. Tyler said his brother Luke might be coming in. I promise, I'm not playing matchmaker. We just learned about it yesterday and he might be here by Friday. Is that okay?"

"Yes, I think I can handle a brother if he's a nice as Tyler."

"I don't know, I've never met him, only seen pictures."

Friday came and Lucy finished pulling the cookies out of the oven. She arranged them on the dish she used to bring them to dinner.

She decided to leave Maximo, her puppy, at home to give her a reason to leave early if she needed it. She jumped into her old truck and drove the one and a half miles to the entrance to Ramona's ranch. She didn't see any other cars and figured that Luke hadn't made it.

As usual, she walked into the kitchen door, smiling. She didn't see Ramona but a man wearing a cowboy hat was reaching up into the cabinet to grab a glass. His other arm was in a sling. He slowly turned.

Lucy dropped her plate of cookies, the ceramic dish shattering on the tiled floor. "Ryan?"

"Lucy?"

Ramona ran into the kitchen. "What's wrong?"

Lucy shook her head and backed up. "No. No. No! You're dead. You can't be here." She turned, ran to her truck, and peeled out of the driveway.

Ramona looked at Luke. "What did you do to her?"

Luke, coming out of his shock, ignored her question and headed toward the door.

Ramona stopped him. "Luke, don't be stupid. Let her cool down from whatever it is."

"That's her," was all he said.

"What do you…Oh." Ramona remembered Tyler telling her something about Luke meeting a mysterious woman.

"I have to go after her. To explain."

"Hold on, cowboy. Look, I don't know what you did to her or why she ran, but she was pretty messed up emotionally when she got here."

"I didn't do anything. She disappeared on me."

He moved toward the door, but Ramona stepped in front of him. "Not so fast, cowboy. Let her be for a while. If I know Lucy, she'll need to process seeing you before she can talk about it. I'll text her and we'll take it one step at a time."

"But I need to explain."

"Yes, you do, to me too. Especially why she called you Ryan."

Ramona walked out of the kitchen in search of Tyler. They needed to figure this out. She texted Lucy while she looked.

"Lucy, are you okay? I don't know what Luke said or did to you, but we'll get to the bottom of it. Text me back when you get home."

Lucy's hand shook as she slammed the truck door and headed to the stables, where she saddled up Frisky. She mounted him, then walked him the two miles to the meadow.

Frisky saw the open field and Lucy felt his excitement.

"Okay, Frisky. Let's go."

When she let him gallop, her mind emptied. The wind whipped at her face, erasing all her stress. It wasn't until she reached the edge of the canyon and the sun slowly slipped from the sky that she slowed and turned back toward her home.

She didn't see the text until after she brushed and fed Frisky, hugged Maximo, and took a shower. She responded simply.

"I'll come over after breakfast."

She shut off her phone, not wanting to see any reply; ate a frozen dinner with a glass of wine; and then binge-watched Friends. She started crying during episode three and fell asleep on the couch after episode four.

The next morning, she couldn't decide what to wear or if she should put on makeup. So instead of making a decision, she went to the barn and brushed Frisky before letting him out into the paddock. Smelling like a horse, with mud on her boots, she jumped into her truck before she could change her mind.

They were just finishing breakfast. Ramona offered her some coffee and she took it.

"Where is he?"

"He just went upstairs before you got here. I'm sure he heard your truck and will be right down. Why don't we sit on the porch."

The porch was Lucy's favorite part of the ranch. It overlooked the paddock with horses roaming freely over Texas Hill Country. You could see the entrance gates to the ranch with the elm trees lining the driveway.

They took their coffee to the porch and waited. Luke came in a moment later, his wet hair sticking to his face.

"Hello, Lucy." He stood still for a moment, waiting.

"Hello R…Luke." She looked down at her hands in her lap.

Ramona stood. "Okay, now that the ice is broken, Lucy, if you want me to stay I will, but I think this is better with just you two. Will you be okay?"

Lucy didn't answer right away but then nodded. "Yes, thanks."

Lucy stared at Luke while sipping her coffee and waited.

Luke sat on the chair next to her and folded his hands. "Why'd you leave me that night?"

Whatever Lucy was expecting, it wasn't that question. She almost slammed the coffee cup onto the table. "What? Why don't you tell me first why you lied. Your name isn't Ryan and you're married."

"What? Married? Where'd you get an idea like that?"

"I saw the photo in your wallet at the hotel room."

It took him a moment to remember. "You thought that was my wedding?"

"Wasn't it?"

"No, it wasn't. The woman in that picture was my step-sister, Georgianna. I was a groomsman."

But it said "Our wedding day."

"I really wish you would have asked me instead of running away. I thought we had something beautiful."

Lucy looked at her lap again. "It was beautiful." A tear slid down her face. "But I was engaged to be married in three weeks."

"Shit. Did you marry him?"

"No, after that night with you, I couldn't. I kept thinking I was a cheating liar just like you. I didn't deserve a good man like Kenny. I left him and I left everyone I knew and came here. What about your name? You haven't told me that yet."

"I was an undercover operative for the FBI. Ryan was my cover."

"So the whole logistics thing and 'we helped the circus' thing was a lie too?"

"I was working for the logistics company before I was approached by the FBI. That wasn't a lie.

"Did your mother really go into the hospital?"

"She did, it's the truth, but not at that time. No, that was the weekend I got shot in the back and the head. You probably remember the scar on my back, but I never showed you this." Luke pushed back his hair and showed her a large scar behind his right ear. "When we met in DC I couldn't tell you that. I was still working. So I reversed the timeline for the two events. But the shooting in the back came first, then I went out to my mom's because she did go into the hospital. Since I was still on leave, recovering from the shooting, I was able to go."

"So, you worked for them until now?"

"Yes, I've been working in the DC office as a researcher the last two years."

"How'd you hurt your arm?"

"Believe it or not, I fell off a ladder in the office. We were repainting the reception area. My forearm broke right in half. I couldn't type and I couldn't work in the field. They offered me a medical out, so I took it and here I am."

Lucy didn't know what to ask next. She had imagined him dead for so many years. Then she thought he was married. Now, here he sat in front of her, single and alive, but named Luke.

He gently put his hand on her thigh and Lucy felt the warmth radiate up her body. "Look, Lucy, I know we weren't together very long and we kind of got a rocky start."

A snort escaped Lucy. "Rocky? Was it even a start?"

"Call it what you want, but the few hours I spent with you, I could never get out of my head. I looked for you, you know."

"I didn't know."

"I guess your brother never told you. After you left me in DC I called the bar. They told me they didn't know where you went."

"Because they didn't. I didn't want anyone following me, trying to make me change my mind. I told them a few months after I moved, but with strict instructions never to tell my ex or anyone else who was looking for me."

"Why? Why did you leave?"

"You know, I don't think you've known me long enough for me to answer that."

"Point taken. But I'd like to get to know you more." He flipped his hand so it was palm up and lifted it as if he wanted to shake her hand. "Hi Lucy, my name is Luke.""

Lucy put her hand in his. "Hi Luke, my name is Lucy."

She stood then and pulled him up with her. "I'm hungry, do you think there is any breakfast left?"

Luke smiled. "Honey, if there isn't anything left, I can cook you a feast.

Lucy pulled him toward the door. "A man who can cook too. How did I get so lucky.

***

Sunday morning, Lucy paid little attention to what she was doing when she saddled Frisky. Her mind was still thinking about the night before. She let him kiss her and it was like a memory coming to life.

She walked Frisky to the meadow and felt Frisky's need to run. This time, Lucy felt as if she galloped toward something instead of running away from it.

She didn't see the feral hog, but Frisky did. When Frisky veered left, it caused Lucy to swing right. The cinch strap wasn't as tight as it should have been and the saddle moved sideways throwing Lucy off the horse. Her head bounced off a rock and she fell unconscious.

Hours later, when Lucy didn't show up at Ramona's house to visit with Luke again, he drove down to hers. He found Frisky eating grass in front of the house with the saddle askew. When he couldn't find her, he went back to Ramona's. He still wasn't able to ride, so Ramona and Tyler, after grabbing the emergency kit, went out looking for her.

When they found her, she was still unconscious.

Ramona inspected her but didn't find any broken bones. However, blood oozed from a large area on the back of her head. She wrapped it using supplies from the kit, then helped Tyler get Lucy draped over the saddle with her head against the horse's mane. Tyler mounted behind Lucy to keep her from falling off and they slowly walked back to the ranch.

They called Luke and had him phone the hospital. The ambulance arrived a few minutes before Ramona and Tyler made it back. They rushed Lucy to the hospital, where she was taken straight to the operating room. Ramona, Tyler, and Luke drove behind the ambulance.

They worked for two hours to stop the bleeding and sew up the wound. After that, they wheeled her to intensive care.

When they heard that she was stable, Ramona and Tyler returned home to care for their horses. Luke waited in the waiting room.

An hour later, her heart monitor alerted the nurses to her cardiac arrest caused by an aneurysm that nobody could have predicted. They couldn't save her.

Meant to Be

Destined to Love

*T*he post office where I work is in the middle of nowhere, Alabama, and when a letter arrived addressed to Theresa Markup at an abandoned farmhouse, it just begged to be opened.

I've never been one to break the rules, but sometimes you got to bend them. Like the time a letter came here for Gertie Malone. She had been dead for five years. As acting postmaster, I figured it was my duty to make sure it wasn't important before I returned it.

Good thing I did, too, because that envelope had five hundred dollars cash tucked in a card that said, "Sorry this is late. Love, Earnest."

We all heard the lectures from Gertie about never staying with a man who won't pay you back. Gertie dispensed all kinds of un-asked for advice. We didn't think anything of it, but apparently, she gained that knowledge from experience.

I jotted a note to Mr. Barns in California.

Dear Mr. Barns,

I'm sorry to say that Gertie's been gone from this earth for about five years now. You know, Gertie used to tell us, "Never to date a man who doesn't pay you back. Those aren't men, those are snakes." I suppose now, you are no longer a snake.

Gertie's grand and great grandchildren still live here. I don't think you intended on getting the money back since you sent cash in the mail. It could have been stolen by anyone. When they asked me where it came from, I told them, even though I knew you were a former snake, that it was from a long, lost friend who owed her.

It's better late than never, so thank you.

Yours truly,

Gertie's friend.

We never heard back from him. Maybe he fixed all the things he felt guilty about, then croaked. He had to be old since Gertie died at age ninety-two.

Mostly, deceased individuals received junk mail. I clip the coupons and special offers and put them in a bin on the counter.

But this letter from Teresa Markup was different. Who the hell was she anyway and why'd she say she lived at 1 Bison Street, Neelburg, AL? That was the old Murphy place. Nobody's lived there since the Revolution, I think.

The return address showed SFC Gunnerson at an APO, AE address. That meant he could be anywhere in Europe, the Middle East, Africa, or wherever. I couldn't disappoint this poor soldier, so I opened it to figure out what to do.

> *Dear Theresa,*
>
> *I normally don't answer these "Support our Troops" letters but since yours was the last in the box, and all the others had gone, I thought I'd do at least one. I apologize that I can't answer some of your questions.*
>
> *Like, I can't say where I am, for security reasons you know. But I can say, there's a lot of sun and sand here. Sometimes there are wind storms where the sand is whipped up like a hurricane and thrown over everything in its path.*
>
> *But it's not always dry here. One time, the rain came down so hard, the sand turned into rivers that flooded our area only to be bone dry in three days.*
>
> *I also can't say what I'm doing here. But eating bagged food and drinking from a water buffalo is the norm.*
>
> *Do I have friends here? You asked that question of a soldier? We're all buddies. We're in this together, you know? Do I like them? Well, Scott's got a bit of an attitude about being from New York and Davis, he thinks he's God's gift to women. But they are all doing their job and that's all you can ask sometimes. They cover my back and I cover theirs. We're a team, warts and all.*
>
> *I'll quickly answer some of your other questions since I don't have much time. Where am I from? I'm from Denver, I'm 32 years old and I have dark hair and brown eyes.*
>
> *Do I want to get out? I've been in since I was 18. Someday, if the right situation comes along, I might get out, but for now, it's my life.*
>
> *I probably won't ever hear from you again, so I'll sign off now. Have a great life, Theresa Markup.*
>
> *Yours,*
> *SFC Gunnerson*

After I read it, twice, I slumped in my comfy office chair. It wasn't really an "office" chair but a padded chair at a table behind the counter in a small post office.

I couldn't help thinking about that poor soldier having to read mail from a stranger. Didn't he have anyone writing to him? I couldn't send it back saying "addressee does not exist." No way I could do that. Nope, I had to write him back. I had to support the troops, right?

The clock told me that I had about an hour to go. I delivered all the mail earlier. All that I needed to do was sweep. But supporting the troops seemed more important.

I rummaged for some paper and the only thing I found had flowers all over it. I decided to draw army ants holding guns and crawling up and down the stems. I added tanks driving on the leaves. I didn't want SFC Gunnerson to think I was a girly girl.

> *Dear SFC Gunnerson. (Do I have to keep calling you SFC or do you have a first name?)*
>
> *I have to tell you that I ain't Theresa. I don't know who the hell she is, but the letter came to me, so I opened it. If you got a problem with that, then you can complain to the postmaster here. (A lot of good that would do ya since I'm the postmaster, ha ha.)*
>
> *They call me Bobbie because I won't let them call me anything else. And if you ever see me in person, I'll tell you my real first name, but then I'd have to marry you so you'd keep it a secret.*
>
> *Anyhow, the reason I opened the letter is because we don't have any Theresa Markup here and the address is an abandoned house down the road. Why would someone go and write to you soldiers and not tell you who they are is baffling. I guess some of those "Support Our Troops" people get crazy and ask anyone to write a letter or maybe this Theresa was in witness protection. Who's to say?*
>
> *Except for my real first name, I'll tell you all about me.*
>
> *I grew up in Neelburg, Alabama and I'm number 75 in a total population of about 123. It might be 124 by the time you get this since my older sister, Debbie, is about to populate another inhabitant.*
>
> *You might ask why a smart, funny girl like me is still living in this podunk town, and I might answer you that I just ain't felt a need to leave. There's a load of other reasons, but*

they're all boring.

You said you were 32 in your letter. Are you married? Cause if you are, you sure will ruin a great fantasy that I've been having ever since I opened your letter.

But that's okay if ya are. Let me know her address and I'll send her some home-made marmalade (not made by me), and that will be the end of our correspondence.

But if ya aren't…well

Forget it, I ain't going there.

Anyhow, if I want this to go out today, I have to pack it up and send it on its way. The big city collection comes in about ten minutes. If you got time, tell me what's exciting over there, besides army shit.

Take care, SFC Gunnerson and God Bless.

Yours,

Bobbie Bransford (And no, you can't call me BB either.)

P.S. You can keep using that address, since I'm the one that delivers it, I'll know who it's for.

I had just finished licking the envelope when Doug, the mail collector from Huntsville, came through. "Hi, Bobbie."

"Hi, Doug. You're early today."

"We have a new temp and sorting went a bit faster." He picked up a bag from the counter. "Is this all then?"

"No, there's this." I held up the envelope and started lifting myself out of my chair.

"No need to get up." He reached around the counter and plucked it from my fingers.

I gritted my teeth. "I'm not helpless, you know."

"Don't I know it and will never forget it. But sometimes, Bobbie dear, you need to let a man be a gentleman. It's good for our sensitive egos."

"Ha, sensitive my ass."

Doug laughed and stuffed the letter into the muslin bag with the others. "Okay, Bobbie, I'll see you on Monday afternoon."

"See ya." Doug didn't make the thirty-minute-long trip on Saturdays, unless I called with urgent mail. So far, that's never happened.

Closing time came soon after Doug left. I hobbled around with my cane locking windows and doors, not that it was necessary since there wasn't much to steal here, but the ritual got my brain in the right frame of mind to go home.

While I work, delivering mail in my adapted Jeep and hanging around the post office to help people, I feel useful. But at home, a mother-in-law suite at my sister Debbie's house, I get smothered. I know she loves me, but I can do things on my own now. I avoid home, by first going to the bar for dinner and a beer. Sometimes I stay and play a game of pool or darts with the regulars, which I guess includes me now. But when I get home, she runs out to the Jeep to inspect me and make sure I ain't suffering.

Tonight isn't any different, even though she's as round as a beach ball with a baby that's about to pop. "Bobbie, how are you doing?"

"I'm doing the same as I always am, Debbie, I'm fine. You need to stop worrying about me and worry about that little one coming soon."

"Well, George and I want to talk to you about that. Do you have a minute before you go in for the night?"

George is a well-meaning man and he loves my sister. But he's also after getting anything for free that he can. It made me nervous that he wanted to talk.

"Sure, I'll follow you in." We both waddled into the house.

George was sitting on the couch with a beer but jumped up when we walked in. "Hi Bobbie, how ya doing?"

"I'm doing just dandy and yourself?"

"I've got a predicament and I need you to do something for me."

"Oh, what's that?" I feared the worst.

George looked at Debbie and then me. "My mother is leaving my father and wants to come here and watch the baby for us."

Relief washed over me. "Well, I'm sorry she's leaving your dad, but it will be good for y'all to have a second person to help with the baby."

George relaxed. "I'm glad you feel that way. She'll be here in two days and that should give you enough time to find a new place, temporarily of course."

I was about to say that was terrific, then it hit me. I flipped my head to look at Debbie. "Find a place? What does he mean, find a place?"

George walked over and put his arm around Debbie. "Just that. We need you to find a temporary place to live while my mom uses the in-law suite to figure things out."

I wobbled over to the couch, carefully set my cane aside, and stared at them. "How long have you known she was coming?"

Debbie sat down on the chair across from me. "Bobbie, she called last night and seemed desperate. Before I could say anything, George told her she could stay in your place." She pushed a piece of paper at me. "I called around today and several folks are willing to put you up for the time being."

The list consisted of Mave, Jerry, and Dawn. Mave, I knew, had a room that she used as one of those hotel things. But Mave had cats and I was allergic. Jerry lived with his brother and there's no way I was moving in with those two horny old men. Dawn smoked cigarettes the way I ate peanut M&Ms. I wasn't about to deal with that kind of smell. Ew.

I pushed the list back across the table. "Debbie, I love you, but you know darn well none of those options will work for me." Before George could respond with anything, I held up my hand and continued. "I've been thinking for a while that I needed to find my own place, and though I didn't think it would happen this soon, it's time I did. I'll call around."

I grabbed my cane and stood too quickly. I saw George reach for me but managed to steady myself before he could come to the rescue. "I'm fine." I took a few steps toward the door and turned. "Look, I get it. I'm not mad or anything. I'll find a place, don't worry. You guys just worry about that little Billy or Susie you got in there."

Debbie ran over and hugged me. "You're the best sister ever."

"I'm your only damn sister, and quit squeezing me so hard."

I walked out the door, across the driveway, and into my apartment. I looked around the small, one room, one bath space and estimated how long it would take to move. I could probably do my clothes and stuff in one trip. I'd have to ask someone to help move my cross trainer. I couldn't live without that, it's the only way I was able to continue walking.

I grabbed another beer and sat down with my phone. There were two real estate agents in town. That, to me, was overkill in a town our size, but the competition between them helped lower prices. I called Jessy's number first.

She answered quickly. "Hello?"

"Hi Jessy, it's Bobbie. Look, something's come up and I need to find a house to move into. Are there any open right now?"

"Oh, you mean because George's mother is coming to town?"

"How did you know about that already? I just heard of it."

Jessy sighed, "George told Michael at the garage this morning. I think probably half the town knows, but we didn't know for sure where she would be staying. I would've called you earlier but figured it would be better to wait, just for a little."

Bobbie sighed. Gossip in small towns spreads like wildfire, which meant that everyone would be stopping by the post office in the morning. Normally, Saturday mornings were quiet, but they wouldn't be tomorrow.

Well, she'd put a stop to all that and just not turn up. "Okay, tell me about what you got."

"There's a darling little place just past Mave's house."

"You mean the old Johnson place?"

"Yep, that's the one."

"Nope, next. "

"Well, there are only two more. The cottage behind Joe's and the apartment behind the bar in town."

I cringed. Neither of those were good options either. "Are there any rentals?"

"Not right now, but maybe we can persuade an owner to rent to you temporarily? "

"Give me time to think and I'll call you back." I hit the "end call" button and scrolled to Gail's number.

It took her two rings to answer but when she did, I knew why. After she said, "Hello," I heard children screaming in the background.

"Stop that right now!" There was a crash and a cry, then Gail got back on the phone. "I'm sorry, Bobbie, the kids were acting up. I've got a few things for you."

I laughed to myself. Not only did she know I would call, but she had things lined up. "If it's the place past Mave's, the bar, or the cottage, I'm not interested."

Gail's pep left her voice. "So, you called Jessy first?"

"Only because her name comes before yours on my phone."

Gail lowered her voice. "Look. I knew I had to have something different in case that happened. The old Murphy place is finally for sale. It's not common knowledge and it's not listed yet, but the grandkids don't want to keep paying taxes on it and they called me a few days ago about listing it."

"I can't live there, it's a wreck."

"Hear me out. I went over there to look at the place, to get an idea of what to list it as. You're right, the house is in shambles, but there is a bunkhouse behind it that's in rather decent shape. I had the water and electric turned on and all it would need is a good dusting. We could help you with that. Then you could take your time and have the main house renovated."

"How much?" I braced myself for a figure that I wouldn't want to pay.

"Well, there's at least three acres of good farm land, and…"

"How much?"

Gail recited the price with a question mark at the end. "A hundred and fifty thousand?"

I've known Gail my entire life and she's one sassy sales lady, but she's also out to get the highest commission. I had to play dirty. "Hmm, that's way too much for a place that's a mess even if it's got a lot of land. Let me call Jessy back and see what she might have found."

"No, don't call her. Please."

"Alrighty, Gail, now give me an answer you know I can deal with."

"Fine. The Murphys are willing to let it go for 75,000 dollars. Tack on my 10 percent and we can make it a deal."

"I want to do an inspection tomorrow morning before I say yes or no."

"I can pick you up at 10 a.m."

"Nope, I'll drive myself there at 7 a.m."

"Ah shucks, have a heart."

"You don't need to be there until 8. I want to have a look around on my own."

"Bless your soul for the extra hour, Bobbie. I'll see you at 8."

"Until then." I pressed "end." I had just enough energy to get ready for bed, then I fell fast asleep. I woke the next morning at 5 a.m. My muscles never let me sleep for long. I stretched, got coffee, and after eating a bagel and taking a couple of aspirin, I stretched again with resistance this time.

By the time I got to the Murphy place, I felt like my normal, but wobbly, self. My legs weren't always trustworthy, so I always carried my cane.

The driveway and yards had recently been cut. Probably Gail's doing before she even came out to the place. She had a terrible fear of snakes and critters. We all used to use it against her growing up. I certainly appreciated not having to negotiate through tall grass.

I walked around slowly. I didn't bother with the front door since I knew it would be secured, but as I passed rusty cans, and newer cans of beer tossed in the yard, I knew that the house may not have been lived in, but it was being used from time to time.

When I got to the back of the house, I noted the boarded-up back door and two windows to either side that had partial boards on them. That's the entry point, I assumed, for all the folks with the beer cans.

About a hundred feet from the house, several buildings stood. An old barn, what looked like a smoke house, and another, square building. I assumed the square building was the bunkhouse. I dodged rusting farm equipment and other debris as I headed to it.

Fortunately, this building had not been encroached upon by anything other than weeds. The windows were also boarded, so I couldn't peek inside.

I walked past it to see the rest of the land. Rolling hills greeted the sun as it rose further into the sky. Gail wasn't kidding when she said it had great pasture land. The fenced-in field of wildflowers and grass looked to be about two feet high. I admired the view for quite a while before I heard a car pull up to the house and I headed back.

Gail was definitely not a morning person, but she did her best to be cheerful. "Morning, Bobbie."

"Good morning, Gail. Thanks for coming out so early."

"I should thank you for letting me escape that crazy house of kids." She pulled keys out from her jeans pocket. "Wanna see inside the house?"

"In a minute, can we see the bunkhouse first?"

"Sure."

She opened the padlock that was across a piece of plywood on hinges, then swung it open. The actual door was in great shape. It looked like the door of a cottage, not a bunk house. She inserted the key and it opened easily.

The place was the size of four of my apartments and had a huge shower in the bathroom. A set of bunk beds lined each corner.

Gail walked over to a cupboard. "I guess this is where they put all their gear, but you can put dishes in here and we can outfit it with an electric stove for now." She pointed to an old cast-iron radiator. "I called Garret and he came out to check the water heater and see if the radiator still worked. He flushed it and said it would do. And we can get you a window A/C unit for the summer."

I did the math in my head. I wouldn't have to dig far into the money I got from the accident. I could use a portion of it as a large down payment, making the monthly mortgage payments smaller. I never let on to anyone how much money the trucking company gave me, but I could've bought a mansion. I didn't need one of those, and the bunkhouse seemed perfect.

I turned my head, eyeing the room and trying to look like I was still thinking on it. "Well, it seems okay. I'd have to knock out a set of those bunk beds over in that corner so I can put my bed in, and then knock those other ones out to make space for my gym." I ran my fingers along a windowsill. "Then I'd have to hire cleaners because I couldn't do it myself." I turned away quickly and pretended to almost fall down. Gail ran over to catch me, but I righted myself before she reached me. Two can play at this game.

Gail saw the twinkle in my eye and smiled. "How about I get my team in here to do the cleaning and your George can take down the extra bunks."

"How soon could I move in."

"The soonest is about thirty days."

I must have looked aggrieved over this because she quickly added, "But I'm sure the Murphys would allow you to rent it for a month before you own it."

I closed the distance between us and put out my hand. "Then Gail, we have a deal."

Sometimes I hated how quickly gossip moved in this town, but then again, it could also be a good thing. By the end of the day, I had a thirty-day rental agreement and a contract on the property. The town gathered together and took care of everything. All the yard debris had been bulldozed to one side of the yard. The bunkhouse was spotless, I had a stove, my bed and all my equipment had been moved in, and tiny details were taken care of by Gail and Debbie. A fluffy bathroom rug matched the toilet seat cover. Flowers sat on the windowsills, and a few pots and pans, donated by townsfolk, lined the shelves. I felt loved.

Everyone had gone except Gail, Debbie, and George when Debbie's water broke. Gail, the expert at having kids, stayed calm while the rest of us went berserk. Eventually, we got Debbie and George into their car with a packed bag and on their way to the next town over that had a hospital.

I drove back to my apartment and made sure all my stuff was out. After removing the last few photos from the wall, I went into Debbie's side and made sure nothing was left on the stove. I turned on the outside lights in case they returned late the next day.

When I got back to my new home, I saw that someone had done me another favor. They had lined a path to the bunk house from the driveway with solar lights. I was so thankful I lived in this town.

Settling in had some drawbacks. I had to buy a new refrigerator since the little one that had been used by farm hands died the first day. Then I bought way too much food at the grocery store and about killed myself going back and forth to the car at night. So I bought a small wagon and kept it next to the driveway to cart them all at once.

I realized that I picked the wrong corner for my bed. It was too far away from the bathroom. That made it difficult to get there in the middle of the night on my rubbery legs. I feared I would fall on my ass.

But, after bribing the bar regulars with pizza and beer, they turned my apartment around for me in about an hour.

Debbie came back from the hospital with a beautiful, eight-pound, blond-headed Billy. George, proud father that he was, delighted in having visitors come to the house. I stopped by every day to see if Debbie needed a hand, but she seemed to drift right into motherhood without any training whatsoever.

It was about two weeks later, on a Friday, when the letter arrived. I did a double take when I saw it addressed to me at my new address. I had been so busy setting up house and playing with my nephew that I forgot all about SFC Gunnerson.

I stopped sorting the rest of the mail and tore it open.

> *Dear Bobbie,*
>
> *I'm sure glad you're not Theresa, she's probably some old nun somewhere. (Who's going to hell 'cause she lied.) I promise, I won't ever ask about your real name unless I'm planning to ask you to marry me. And yes, I could do that because I'm not married.*
>
> *I used to be, but after my first year of deployment I got a Dear John letter. I don't blame her much. We were both really young and she couldn't stand being alone all the time. It wasn't fair to keep going off to wherever Uncle Sam sent me (places where spouses were not allowed to come) and I wasn't about to get out. The lifestyle suited me.*
>
> *In retrospect, I guess we didn't really love each other or it would have lasted like my CO's. He's been married thirty-five years now.*
>
> *I've never been to Alabama. I've actually never been in any other state but Colorado. Traveling around the US is something I've always wanted to do.*
>
> *I'll assume that resident 124 has arrived. Please extend my congratulations to your sister.*
>
> *You never told me what you look like or how old you are. I sure hope you're not some old lady on a rocker. I tell you what, if you send me a photo, I'll send one too.*
>
> *But if you don't want to, that's fine. You seem easy to talk to and that's all that matters. Here's a few more quick questions. Do you own a dog? What's your favorite flower? High heels or sneakers? Filet mignon or pizza?*
>
> *You're a good artist. I loved the ants.*
>
> *I've got to go so I'll sign off and seal this up.*
>
> *Yours,*
> *David*
>
> *For the record, my full name is David William Gunnerson.*

I read the letter three times, pressed it to my heart, then read it again. I ignored the sorting and wrote back right away.

Dear David,

While I love sitting on a porch in a rocker, I usually do it after a long day of work with a beer in my hand. I'm twenty-eight, five six and a half (the extra half makes me taller than my sister), and I have brown hair and greenish brown eyes.

No dog but I'm planning on getting one soon. Camellias, cause they look like roses but are easier to take care of. Boots first. Sneakers second. High heels only if you make me. Pizza covered in pepperoni, onions, peppers, and jalapenos.

My bald headed nephew, Billy, is already taking over the world. He never cries because he doesn't have to. There's always someone around who will pick him up, sing him a song, or carry him to his mama for dinner and dessert. Thank you for asking.

My turn. Do you like horses? Pool or darts? Jeep or Porsche? And the most important question of all, black coffee or frou-frou shit?

About that photo. I don't have any recent ones. I deliver mail around these parts and everyone knows who I am, but nobody needs to put me on their refrigerator, if you get what I mean. I could pull down the one in the post office glass case, but I look like a starving teenager in that one. I'll get someone to take a picture of me for the next letter, okay? You could send yours first, you know.

I better get back to work before someone walks in here and sees me dawdling.

Until next time,
Bobbie

I took a little more time to draw pictures of horses galloping around the edge of the paper, then I sealed and stamped the letter. I had to get the mail sorted and delivered before Doug got here to do his Friday pickup.

Later, before going to the bar for dinner, I changed into my favorite shirt, washed my face, and pulled out my lip gloss, which was about the only makeup I ever used. I checked to see if my phone was charged and headed out.

I ordered my usual stout beer and a burger, then handed Jimmy my phone. "Jimmy, take my picture, would you?"

"Why do you want me to do that?"

"Don't ask. It's some stupid work thing." Okay, it wasn't really work, but it was for a letter, which is mail, and by default work, right?

"Okay, smile."

I barely had time to say cheese when he took the picture and handed back my phone. I glanced at it, figured it would do, then proceeded to enjoy my meal while I thought about David with the dark brown hair and brown eyes. When I got home, I uploaded the picture to a print place at the drug store. It said it would take about four or five days to get back to me.

Just before I fell asleep, it dawned on me that we could be emailing each other. I didn't like the idea. It seemed too personal and I didn't know this guy. Plus, I enjoyed getting letters, so, unless he said otherwise, I wasn't going to bring it up.

The next few weeks flew by. I spent as much time with Billy as I could. Not only to give Debbie and George a break, but because I loved kids. It was bittersweet being with him, but I loved him. I couldn't have children because of the accident that crushed my legs and damaged my uterus so bad they had to remove it.

Before the accident, I worked part time as a courier, not a real postal employee, but I did the same things. There wouldn't be any mail service at all in Neelburg if the town hadn't purchased the building, negotiated a contract with USPS, and paid me from their funds. Folks used to drive all the way to Huntsville to get their mail, but the Mayor decided he had enough of that. I drove my own jeep to Huntsville three days a week to pick it up. Doug came down to us on Mondays and Fridays.

I did this for about three years before my accident. They didn't have anyone to take my place and so the townsfolk took turns doing the job while I recovered.

When I got out of the hospital, they had fixed and altered my Jeep. My legs weren't able to push the gas and brakes for a long time, so they added that capability to the steering wheel. Then they added a revolving cart so after I sorted, I didn't have to reach into the back to get the last few pieces. I just turned the bin like spinning the wheel on Wheel of Fortune.

My legs work almost as good as new now, but I limp and, if I'm walking too much or standing too much, they get tired, so I appreciate all the help the town gives me.

I was about to give up on SFC Gunnerson. Five weeks passed with no letter, then I got two on the same day. The back of one of the envelopes had the number one written on it and a note that said "Please open number one first." The other envelope had a number two on it. The note said to wait for letter number one and read number one first. I opened letter one.

Dear Bobbie,

Congratulations on Billy. I bet he's cute.

I don't drink anything but black coffee. Besides, they don't have any "frou-frou shit" where I am. I love horses and took riding lessons when I was a kid, but I haven't been on a horse for over fifteen years. Do you ride?

You ask about pool and darts as if you know a lot about them. I'm pretty good at eight-ball and might say that I can usually hit what I'm aiming. As for darts? I throw grenades with more accuracy.

You'd never catch me in a jeep. I guess I'm in them too often over here. I left behind a 1949 Dodge pickup that I'd like to restore one day. Every now and then on leave, I take it out of my mom's garage for a spin. She's nice enough to keep it for me. The engine's in good shape, as I did all that work whenever I visited, but the outside of it is a mess and needs much TLC.

If you gave me a Porsche, I wouldn't turn it down, but I'd not buy one.

The picture I enclosed is from my promotion two years ago. I look the same. I'm the handsome one in the middle, the big lug on my left is Sergeant Scott, and the one on the right is Sergeant Davis. I mentioned them before. You're only the second person to get a copy of this picture. The other went to my mom in Denver.

Instead of questions this time, I'm going to tell you more about myself, then you can do the same. I love lying in freshly mowed grass and looking at the stars. You know, there are people over here who have never seen grass like ours in America. Lush and green with a sweet smell that reminds me of lemonade stands and the fourth of July.

In my forever home, I want to live near water. I've gone several days with just drops of water and thought I would die. It can be near an ocean, a lake, or my big backyard pool.

Life is short. You never know when something will change. At the end of each day, I think of something good that happened. Even if the only thing I can think of is that I let an ant live instead of squashing it.

Your pizza sounds terrific but I'd add bacon and sausage.

It's late and I got a big day tomorrow. I'll try to get this out.

Yours,
David.

I couldn't believe how wonderful he sounded. Was he for real? I ripped open letter number two. The writing was different, not as neat as before.

Dear Bobbie,

I'm so sorry I haven't written and it looks like my previous letter never made it off my night stand so I'll send these out together. Maybe you'll get them the same day but no matter, I numbered them so you'd read the other one first.

The fact that I'm writing this means that I survived. You see, the day after I wrote letter number one, I had spinal surgery to remove shrapnel that had lodged there six months before when a bomb went off near our guard post. I was in a coma for three weeks before that, and when I woke, I couldn't move my legs.

I had other injuries that the doctors attended to first before they could even think about doing the surgery. My mind was in a terrible place for a while. I thought about doing myself in. And then I got the letter from Theresa. I'll admit now, that I didn't want to write that letter, but my buddies told me I had to. I'm glad I did.

Your voice sounded so fresh. So alive. I dreamed of your letters, even though there were only two.

In the last letter I said that you never know when something will change. Well, for me, the surgery the next day could have had several outcomes. I had no choice. If I left the shrapnel in, I'd be paralyzed for life. That would have been awful enough, but there was always the looming possibility that it would move and pierce an organ or something else. It could kill me just by being inside me.

The surgery had risks as well. My doctor said the best case scenario would be that the pressure on my spine would be relieved when the metal was removed which could mean I'd feel my legs again. The risk of complete paralysis or death, however, was high.

It's been two weeks since the surgery and I'm finally able to sit up a little bit and hold a pen. They still don't want me moving too much, but at least I know I still can. I don't know about my legs though since the bottom half of my body is in a cast.

It's taken me two days to write this much and I really want to get this to you. I will understand if you don't want to keep writing to me given my possible future situation. But I want to say that it's been good chatting with you, even just a little bit.

Yours
David

It wasn't until the paper started getting wet that I noticed I was crying. I felt his pain. I felt his despair, and I felt his hope. I'd been there. What were the chances that I'd get his letter? It's like it was meant to be. I quickly pulled out my paper and started writing.

That's it, SFC Gunnerson. I order you to call me or email me as soon as you get this. My number is 205-444-8423. My email is Bobbieb1212@gmail.com. Let me tell you a story.

Three years ago I got hit by a Semi. I was delivering mail and the truck took a corner too fast. It hit the back of the jeep while I was standing in front of the passenger side. The truck pushed the jeep over my legs, crushing both. I had five broken bones in one leg and three in the other. My pelvis was cracked in three places and I had internal bleeding.

Fortunately, the trucker made it and called 911. I spent a long time in the hospital not knowing if I'd ever walk again. I also lost any ability to have children.

But that's all in the past. I walk with a limp and have to use a cane just in case my legs give out, which they do from time to time. If I don't stretch all my muscles and do my exercises each day, I lose some mobility.

All that to say, I've been there, done that. So, David William Gunnerson, call me!

If you don't call me, I'll hunt you down.

Bobbie.

I wished I had more information on him. I wanted to call up his unit and find him. I mailed the letter Express Mail and hoped to hear from him soon.

I hadn't told anyone about my two letters to David. I felt such a connection and I wanted to keep it to myself. But when I stopped in to see Billy on my way home, Debbie could tell something was up.

"Why do you have that look on your face?"

I moved my gaze from Billy, who was asleep in my arms, to Debbie.

"What look?"

Debbie pointed at me. "The look you always gave your physical therapist when you said you were okay. The look that turned to pain once he left. C'mon, spill. Are you hurting?" She reached out to take Billy.

I hugged him closer. "You could always read me like a book. No, I'm not hurting. Not any more than my normal aches and pains. It's personal."

"Do I have to squeeze it out of you or are you going to tell me." Debbie put her elbows on her knees. She looked like a tiger ready to pounce. "Is it the house? Is something wrong?"

"You won't give up, will you?" I leaned forward and pulled the last two letters from my back pocket. "I opened a letter to some stranger that was addressed to the Murphy house. Turns out it was a soldier's response to one of those letters people write to any soldier to give them a lift, you know the ones I mean?"

Debbie nodded. "Yes, go on."

"We'd written about two letters back and forth…"

Debbie interrupted. "Oh my! You like this guy."

I turned my head to avoid her eyes. "No, I don't. I mean yes, but not like you're thinking. I'm just doing my part to help support the soldiers."

"Okay, sure. Keep going. That's not worrisome. What happened?"

I didn't know what to say, so I handed her the letters. She read them in order. I saw tears in her eyes before she finished letter number two.

"What are you going to do?"

"What I want to do is call him but I have no idea how to find him. He could be anywhere in the world with that APO address and he hasn't given me any idea where he is. I wrote him a letter and gave him my phone and email. I guess we just wait."

Debbie jumped up pulling out her phone. She dialed the mayor at his home. "Hello, Scott. I'm sorry to call you on your cell phone, but this is an emergency."

I tried to get her to stop. "What are you doing? It's not an emergency."

She hushed me and continued. "No. Nobody's hurt. It has nothing to do with anyone in town. Bobbie has a soldier friend that needs our support. Can we call in the team for a meeting tomorrow at the post office?"

I slapped my forehead. I knew there was a reason I didn't tell anyone. But then I remembered. During recovery, Debbie had organized the embrace I got from the entire town. The visits, the gifts, and the cards all helped me stay positive. My sister, though a pain in the ass sometimes, knew how to hand out love. I smiled at her and gave her the thumbs up.

The next day, near closing time, Debbie, Mayor Briggs, Gail, Jessy, and our town librarian, Kate, all joined me at my table behind the counter.

Debbie thanked them all for coming, then looked at me. "Tell them the story, Bobbie."

I told them. Then I read letter number two aloud to them.

Gail spoke first after rubbing her eyes. "Oh, that poor man. I'll start right away letting everyone know to donate something."

"What kinds of things should we tell them we need?" Jessy pulled out her phone to start a list.

Mayor Briggs pulled out his phone and searched for what can be sent to APO addresses. He read the list aloud. "Sunblock, socks, underwear, flip-flops, lip balm and powder. Snacks, including chips, salsa, nuts, cookies, beef jerky, non-melting candy and trail mix in packaging that isn't easily crushed. Drink mixes in single-serving packets are also a good addition."

Kate looked appalled. "Why would they need flip-flops and doesn't the Army give them enough sunblock? Goodness, don't they take care of their own soldiers?"

Mayor Briggs laughed. "Yes, they do. The stuff they give you works, but it ain't pretty smelling or looking. At least that's what I remember."

I crossed my arms. "I'm not asking folks to buy underwear either. That just seems stupid. What about games? We could buy lots of games. I remember being bored to death in that hospital bed."

"I like that idea," Kate said.

"Okay then, snacks and games it is." Jessy wrote down the list.

Gail interrupted her. "Wait. Isn't he in a hospital? It won't be right to send things only to David. Let's make sure we have enough for everyone. I think more games than snacks too, 'cause they might not allow them to eat the snacks. You know how hospitals are about outside food."

Bobbie snickered. "Right, I remember. Let's send them anyway. Maybe the staff can eat them if David and the other patients can't."

Debbie was about to end the meeting for all when she realized. "Hey, are we sending all of this to David's APO address? It seems like a lot. Will he even get it in the hospital. I wish there was a way to find out what hospital he's in."

"I'll see if I can find out if that's possible. But I doubt we'll get any information since none of us are relatives." Mayor Briggs didn't look hopeful.

I said, "I hope he calls me before we have the care packages assembled. Then I can ask him where to send it."

We all agreed that the post office would be the collection area. Jessy said she'd bring in a few packing boxes after she looked up size limits for mailing to APOs.

After three days I got anxious. Doug said that people from Huntsville who send letters to their loved ones at APOs are always complaining about how long it takes, even for Express Mail. I knew I should be patient, but that didn't stop me from checking my email every thirty minutes or making sure my phone was turned up as loud as it could be so I wouldn't miss a call.

When I walked up to the post office the next day, there were boxes and bags all over the front porch. "I'm going to have to call in the troops for this."

I unlocked the door and, as soon as I sat down to check my laptop email, my phone rang.

"What now?" I grumbled as I pulled it out of my pocket. I didn't recognize the number and I didn't recognize the area code. My heart sped up. "Hello?"

"Hi, My name is SFC David Gunnerson, may I please speak to Bobbie Bransford?"

My voice squeaked. "David. I'm so glad you called!"

Laughter came through the phone. "When a woman orders you to call her, you must obey. But seriously, before we talk about anything else, thank you. You have no idea how much your letter, well all three of your letters, have meant to me."

"You may change your mind when year hear what's coming."

"Oh yeah? Bring it on."

"Folks in my town caught wind that you were in the Army and in the hospital. You've turned into a local cause. You have one chance to hang up now before armasnackatoydon descends upon your hospital room."

"Armaasnack-ah-what?"

I laughed and tried to explain. "David, when my sister found out that I actually wrote a real letter, to a man no less, she added one plus one and had us going down the aisle already. Anyway, that's just to warn you. The rest of the town decided they agreed with her and started a collection for you while you're stuck in the hospital. And because you're in an Army hospital with a bunch of other soldiers that might need cheering up, well let's just say that the amount of stuff you're going to get is sinful. Just sinful. Now, where should I send all of this? Do you know the hospital's address?"

Silence greeted me, then the low rumble of laughter filled the phone. "Bobbie, you are something else. If any other woman would talk to me about even thinking about getting married, I'd turn her around and send her out the door. But you make me laugh and I want to laugh more. I'll email you the hospital address and the room we're in. Hey, can you do a video call? I need to show you all my warts so that you will stop trying to get me to that church.”

I hit the FaceTime icon and then there he was. The jagged scar above his beautiful brown eyes still had stitch marks. His smile created dimples on his cheeks, the left one being speared with another scar that made it look like cupid’s arrow. The brown fuzz on his head matched the fuzz on his chin.

“Well, I am speechless. Bobbie, you are beautiful. I had prepared myself for the bride of Frankenstein and I get Miss America.” David whistled. “Bobbie, I am so glad you answered that letter.”

“Well, Mr. SFC Gunnerson, you ain’t so bad to look at yourself. Let me see the rest of you?”

David turned his phone. The rest of his body was under a sheet. When he turned it back to his face he said, “There’s not much to see, as you can see. We’ll save that for the big reveal later.”

I softened my voice. “David, I am so sorry you are going through this. Can you tell me how it happened?”

David gave me a brief outline of the event. Before we knew it, an hour had passed by. We only noticed the time because Sergeant Scott entered the room and stole the phone from David. “You’re the famous Bobbie, well you’re definitely not an old woman in a rocking chair like he said you were. Just so you know, I’m always available if this fleabag doesn’t work for you. I’m going to put the phone down a minute, set up his phone, then give you back to him.

I stared at the ceiling for about a minute and then David came back. He had earphones in this time. “I’m back. Scott just came to say goodnight to me. He’s got a mission to run. He also set up my phone so I could keep FaceTiming you but be hands free. My arm gets so tired trying to hold up the phone for so long.”

Another thirty minutes went by. We talked like friends that have been together for years. I had no shy episodes, and his laughter made my heart flutter. I could tell that exhaustion had caught up to him when his eyelids started covering those big eyes of his.

“David, you are getting tired and I need to let you go and rest. Please, I know the nurses can be a pain in the ass, but listen to them, it’s for your own good.”

David just nodded.

“You can email me the hospital’s address in the morning. Get some sleep. Okay?”

A soft “okay” was followed by the face of a nurse.

“Hello, Bobbie is it? You’re all he’s talked about. Anyway, he’s almost asleep, so I’m going to say goodbye to you and put his phone away.”

"Thank you." I ended the call.

In the morning, I received an email from David.

Dear Bobbie,

OMG what a horrible date I am, falling asleep on the call. Good thing nurse Ratchet caught my phone before it fell to the tile floor and blew up.

Did I say date? Sorry, I hope you don't think that too forward of me, but you are all I think about besides bed pans, itchy skin under my cast, and getting poked and prodded by the nurses. And now that I know what you look like, I can't stop seeing you in my head. (At least I think that's you, these drugs are pretty strong.)

I feel like I could talk to you all day and would do just that if I called you. But I know you have a busy life, you're not stuck in a bed, so I'll let you do the calling when you are available.

Now that I know you aren't some foreign spy trying to figure out where the troops are, I can tell you where I am. I'm in Landstuhl Regional Medical Center. They flew me here when I woke from my coma and I've been here so long that I know all the nurses' marital statuses, their hometowns, and their favorite foods. (And I know that because they sneak some to me now and then. It's one of the advantages of being one of the more handsome soldiers.) Have you ever had a German Brotchen or pretzel? Dipped in mustard they are sooo good. It's almost up there with pizza.

Typing all this using my phone is tiresome and nurse Ratchet (the only one who hasn't fallen for my charm) is here to give me a bath. Oh joy!

Just send all packages to my APO address that you already have. I'll have Scott and a couple of the guys bring it out here. That way they can enjoy some of it as well. How much should we expect?

Anyway, I'm being attacked by sponges while I type. Got to go!

Yours,
David

I couldn't believe my eyes. Did he really say we were dating? I read it again. Yep, that's what he said. I got up and used my phone to take a picture of the six boxes that were already packed and ready to go, then I took one of the piles of stuff that people had left there overnight. I attached them to my reply email.

> *Dear David,*
>
> *You must be squeaky clean by now. I remember those baths. Make sure Nurse Ratchet keeps her hands where they are supposed to be.*
>
> *I agree, that was the worst date I've ever been on. You'll have to make it up to me in person if you ever come stateside. But, the good thing is, I enjoy talking with you too and you're easy on the eyes, so I reckon I'll continue.*
>
> *I do got to get to work now, but let's just set a time to call. I get off work at around 4:00 but that's really late for you, so why don't we stick to my lunchtime at 12:00 which is, I think, 7:00 for you. I'm in central time, remember. And you should call me. I don't want to wake you if you are sleeping or cause Nurse Ratchet to have to catch your phone again.*
>
> *I'll get the rest of the packages boxed up and send them on their way today. How many boxes? Look at the pictures and you'll know.*
>
> *Talk to you later.*
> *Bobbie*

I started carrying in items from the porch when my phone buzzed with a text message.

> *We're going to need a trailer and the entire platoon to haul that to the hospital. Please tell your town thanks. That's so generous. Talk to you later, I'm about to pass out.*
> *David.*

Texting! We're texting now too! I haven't dated many men, but most of them wouldn't send a text unless you called them to tell them to answer your text. I felt loved already. My response was short.

> *I'll relay the thanks. Sleep well. TTFN*

I added a few sleeping emojis and got to work.

It didn't take long for everyone in town to know, for sure, that I was in a relationship with David. We spoke every day during my lunch hour and texted constantly, one-line jokes or updates, throughout the day.

After several months, I knew I loved David and we said it to each other. I often wonder how I knew, but I did.

I was on the phone with him when he took his first steps on the parallel bars.

I was on the phone with him when he walked on his own.

I screamed at his physical trainer through the phone when those necessary, beautiful monsters made him hurt in order to heal.

We talked every day.

The day David said he would be discharged from the hospital to go to Walter Reed Army Medical Center in DC, I got nervous.

"You're coming home?"

"Yes, Bobbie, I'm coming back to the US. They will assign me to the hospital in DC to continue my physical therapy for a few more months. They will also assess my disability so they can retire me from duty."

"Oh David, I'm so sorry, the military has been your life. What will you do?"

"I am hoping that a beautiful girl from a nowhere town in Alabama will help me with that."

"Oh I get it, you want to come and live off of my income, right?"

David laughed. "When they say I am healthy enough to get out of the Army, I plan to come and redo that first date. We'll take it from there, eh? Know any good places to stay in your little town?"

"What about your mom? Won't she want you to go back to Colorado?"

"I've already spoken to my mom. She's planning to visit me when I get to DC. She knows all about how I feel about you and said I was a grown man and had to do what I had to do."

"I love your mom already."

"I think you'll like her."

A few weeks later, I received a call from a strange number but it had the same area code as David. "Hello?"

"Hi Bobbi, this is Rene, David's mom. He's due to arrive in DC in a week and I wanted to surprise him. Were you planning on meeting him in DC?

"Hello, Ms. Gunnerson. It's nice to meet you. I've thought about meeting him there but hadn't made any plans yet."

"Oh good. I'd like to invite you to join me in surprising him. Does that sound okay?"

"Sure. I love surprises. What do you want me to do?"

"Just make him think that you'll be a week late coming to see him. I'll handle all the rest. Can you get time off from work?"

"I haven't taken a vacation in a while, so that won't be a problem."

"Terrific, I can't wait to meet you in person. Send me your mailing address."

Either I won the lottery or I've met the nicest mother on the planet. Two days later I received a package from Rene. It included a round-trip first-class ticket to Ronald Reagan Washington National Airport, limousine service for a week, and a reservation at the Woodmont Grill.

I picked up my cell called Mayor Briggs.

"Mayor Briggs, this is Bobbie."

"I know, Bobbie, I have caller ID. What's up?"

"I'm going to need to take a week off. Will that be a problem?"

A loud hoot caused Bobbie to remove her phone from her ear. Mayor Briggs finally stopped hooting and said, "He's coming home. Hallelujah. You take as much time as you need, Bobbie. Just let me know the dates and we'll find someone to take over while you're gone."

Bobbie smiled. She loved this town. "Thanks, Scott, I mean Mayor Briggs."

"I keep telling you to call me Scotty."

"I'll do that when I no longer work for you. See you later. I'll email you the dates."

I used the departing and arrival dates on the plane ticket for my vacation dates.

After sending that email, I looked up the restaurant. The menu seemed okay, but the prices screamed dressy. I needed to go shopping.

The day I departed, Debbie said she'd drive me to the airport. Half the town gathered outside her house for our departure and, as we walked to the car, they yelled, "Knock him dead. Give him our love. Hug him like a bear, and bring him home."

I'd never flown in a plane before, and I didn't remember the helicopter ride that took me to the hospital after my accident. First class pampered me with snacks and sodas and there was plenty of room to stretch my legs. I felt bad for the people in economy and made a note to thank Rene even more.

When the plane landed and stopped, I texted Debbie.

"I'm here."

Her response was short. "Go get him." Following that were several heart Emojis.

Even with the extra leg room, my legs felt wobbly and I needed to use my cane. When I exited security, I spied a woman in jeans and a white shirt wearing a cowboy hat. Some of my nerves relaxed.

"Bobbie, over here!"

I hobbled over to where she stood.

She gathered me into a gentle hug, then pulled away with her hands still on my shoulders. "Oh my, when David said you were beautiful, he wasn't kidding. Thank you so much for coming. He's going to be so surprised. I'll tell you all about it in the car to the hotel."

"Yes, ma'am."

"Please, call me Rene. After all, a friend of David's is a friend of mine."

"Yes, ma'am, I mean Rene."

She laughed, helped me get my bags, and whisked me to a limo that waited outside.

During the ride to the hotel, Rene told me that David's plane would arrive tomorrow afternoon. Rene would meet him at the gate and bring him back to the hotel, where Bobbie would be waiting in the adjoining room.

"I'll have ordered room service for your dinner and I'll make myself scarce."

"Oh no, don't you want to be with him too?"

"Bobbie, David is my grown son. I'm not one of those suffocating mothers that needs to be the most important person in his life. Honey, I believe that person is you and if I want my son to be happy, then he needs to see you, not me. Your room is one that adjoins his, so if you're not comfortable with any of this, you can just go to your room, but I know my son and he'll want you to be with him. Are you okay with all that?"

I blushed and turned my head and nodded. It's all I could think about, being alone with David. I wasn't kidding myself that anything romantic would happen, he was still recovering, but I craved time alone with him.

"Rene, I don't know how to thank you. I'd like to pay you back for all of this."

"Nonsense. After my husband died ten years ago, I got so much money from his life insurance and selling his company, that I need excuses to spend it all. David certainly never lets me spend it on him."

"Well, I'm of the same mindset as David. I don't like getting gifts of this magnitude, but I accept your gift. Thank you from the bottom of my heart."

"You are welcome. I'm glad you aren't going to keep insisting you pay me back. Let's make that a rule."

"I'll agree to that, but only if you don't go overboard like this again. It's wonderful, I appreciate all of this, but it's still a lot to take in."

"Okay, fine. I promise not to overwhelm you in the future."

I smiled. I liked Rene. If my mother were alive, I imagined she'd be just like this. I leaned over to hug her.

Later, sitting in the adjoining hotel room, I couldn't relax. David and I told each other so many things, we had no trouble talking with each other, but would seeing him in person change anything? I worried that it might. Like seeing a buttery chocolate cake in a bakery, and after looking at it for twenty or so visits, finally buying a piece only to find out it's bone dry.

I heard his door open and muffled conversation. Then there was a knock at my door. I opened it.

"Bobbie, he's all yours. Dinner will come up around 7 p.m., but I've made sure there were snacks and stuff for you both already in the room. If you need anything, you have my number, but I hope that I won't hear from you until breakfast. Let me know what time you'll come down."

I nodded, then hugged her. I couldn't say anything because my nerves were so tight. She pulled away, turned me around, and nudged me back into the room.

Even though the doors were unlocked, I still knocked.

"Come in."

I walked into the room. "Hello, David."

Sitting at the bottom of the bed, he had been looking at the other door and whipped his head around to me. His face lit up and he tried standing up.

"No, don't get up." I ran over and sat down next to him. He pulled me into a hug and we both cried like babies. I knew then that this man would be mine as long as he would have me.

A smile is easily given

With a few words on a page

Pick up a pen

And write a letter to someone you cherish

Worry No More

Obsessive Love

She gazed at my while I cradled her head in my arms, her beautiful blue eyes bright with tears. Me, the only important thing in her life, her world. Tears for the last love she'd ever know trickled lovingly over my hands.

Ever since Vanessa walked into my twelfth-grade English class, my world changed. Everything I ever did after that, I did for her. To show her how much I loved her.

Of course, at first, she didn't know me. You see, I didn't play football or basketball. Nor did I participate in any clubs or ensembles. Being a nobody garnered teasing and sometimes, the most awful pranks. One day close to Christmas, they taped a sign to my back. Of course, I didn't know why students turned around and called me fruitcake until she plucked the sign off my jacket.

Our eyes connected. That's when I knew I loved her. I couldn't tell her at first. That would scare her away. Nobody liked me. Why should I think she'd be any different. I had to show her.

I started with notes. Simple notes, slipped into her locker, about how beautiful she made the world. A poem about how her smile lit up her face. From afar, I watched her open and read them. Vanessa always looked around, searching for the author. She always smiled.

Time seemed to stand still. I needed to speed up the process. I wrote more notes and found more places to leave them, even going to her house and putting them in her mailbox. Until that day when Beau, her boyfriend and the school's football star, saw me putting one on her car windshield. I earned a broken nose for that one. But there is benefit to tragedy.

The next day, Vanessa closed the gap between us. I thought for sure she'd hear my heart pounding. She gently put her arm on my shoulder and apologized for Beau's stupidity. Then she asked me to stop sending the notes since it aggravated him. She let her hand slide down and took mine. "You're nice, but I have a boyfriend." She let go and walked away.

She thought I was "nice." I smiled. She sees me. The rest would come in time. I needed to up my game.

I attended an elite high school on a scholarship. I didn't have money or a job, so, for the sake of love, I became a thief. It wasn't hard. I tapped into the school computers and shaved a few cents off of everyone's lunch account. Nobody would even notice, for about four months at least, that their account was a few dollars short. No biggie for this crowd. The money went into an LLC that I created and named "Used Books." If anyone saw that in a school account spreadsheet, they probably wouldn't think twice about it.

I made about 110 dollars a week and that allowed me to purchase flowers. I had them delivered, of course, and, to keep from getting another bloody nose, I used a false name when I ordered them. I watched her reactions. It felt good to make her happy.

I could wait for her to return my affections. Persistence always won, didn't it?

I celebrated the fact that her house faced the local park. That allowed me to climb onto the roof of the public restrooms. Conveniently, a large sign hid me. I relaxed with my binoculars and watched. I had a terrific line of sight to her house. The first few deliveries made her giddy. Even the love notes, always unsigned, made her smile.

But Beau kept taking all the credit. I had to stop that, so in the next card, I used one of the poems that I wrote her before. She read it, standing at the front door. I could see her excitement in the way her eyes opened wide and she looked for me, her head swiveling left then right. It made my heart sing that she recognized me by my words. She clutched the message and flowers to her chest, then went inside.

For a few days I basked in that giddy feeling. She remembered my poem. It meant something to her. I had to think of the next step.

I still hadn't come up with a plan until one morning, I saw her arguing with Beau. They were screaming at each other in the back parking lot by the football field. When he grabbed her, something came over me. I dropped my books and ran. "Leave her alone!" I can't say I knocked him over because of my brute strength, but the surprise of it, and a shove from Vanessa, had him falling on the pavement. He hit his head, hard. Without a helmet, it hurt.

"What the hell are you doing?"

My breath came in spurts. "You were hurting her."

He got up. He was very tall. "Yeah, what's it to you?" He shoved me and I fell into the grass.

She saved me that day. "Leave him alone, he's a sweetheart for trying to save me." She turned and walked into the school. He spat on me, then ran after her.

That's when I decided to start working out. I watched videos, learned about protein and what to eat to help me bulk up. Instead of flowers, I invested in some free weights and began a running routine. My love for her got me through those days when I wanted to quit.

Beau's New Year's party was the talk of the school. Everyone who was anyone was going. I wasn't invited, but that didn't stop me from attending. I waited until the alcohol flowed freely, then walked in. I needed to watch her, to ensure her happiness, and to bring in the New Year in the same space as her. I never planned to interfere, but then Beau dropped something into her beer just before she chugged it.

Think, think, think. I couldn't just waltz up to him and demand he let her alone, could I. I kept watching. He held a beer in one hand while his other roamed her body. She tried to stop him. He just laughed.

Fortunately, whenever someone yelled, "Chug, chug, chug," he downed a drink. He couldn't fondle and drink at the same time. The cycle repeated. Grope, drink, grope. Vanessa continued her feeble escape attempts, but he held her prisoner. I knew his intentions and had to stop him.

I ran to the bathroom. Ah, a drug cabinet. I knocked things off the shelves in my haste to find something. Nothing. I ran upstairs and found the master bath. Bingo. Apparently, someone had trouble sleeping. I found a bottle of Ambien, but next to it, a bottle of Vicodin. I poured a few pills from each into a plastic cup, spilling a few on the floor. Then I used the end of a hair brush to break them and poured the powder into my hand. I ran back down the stairs to the keg, dropped the powder inside a cup and filled it. Beau had both of his hands on Vanessa. She tried to remove them, but her delicate hands slid off of his without making a dent.

My blood boiled. I got close enough to the group, put the medicated cup on the table next to his empty one, and yelled, "Chug, chug." Beau looked around for a cup, grabbed the one I set there, and chugged it.

Perfect, now all I had to do was wait and I could help Vanessa get out of there. But Beau had other plans. He grabbed her hands and pulled her. She limped along behind him, like one of those wooden dogs with a string that fell on its side. I guess he felt it too, so he picked her up and headed up the stairs. I wished I had started my body building regimen sooner. My skinny body was no match for Beau's football physique, especially a drunk Beau. I needed to stall them.

Running up the stairs behind them, I pretended to wretch. Beau wasn't as drunk as I thought, because he quickly got out of the way and yelled, "First door on the right."

After passing them, I turned and pretended to dry heave some more. It was an Oscar-worthy performance. When Beau saw who I was, he swore, "Jeeze, even the lowlifes are here." But he didn't want to clean up vomit, so he let Vanessa fall to the stair, propped her so she was sitting, sort of, and then dragged me to the bathroom and slammed the door. That's when I saw the pills on the floor and realized that I should somehow get rid of my fingerprints. I quickly cleaned the outside of the bottles and placed them back into the cabinet. Then I wiped all the surfaces with a wet washcloth. It only took a minute, but that gave Beau enough time to retrieve Vanessa and head to his room.

He slammed the door, but I made it just in time and stopped it from closing with my hand. I almost screamed with the pain, but gritted my teeth and held it in.

I peered through the crack and watched in agony. I wanted badly to go in there and pull him off of her but knew how ineffective that would be. I prayed that the drugs would take effect before he could do anything.

My poor love begged for her freedom. "Stop, I don't want to. Remember, I want to wait."

"Oh, c'mon baby, you know you want to. I feel it when you kiss me. Just kiss me, okay. I promise that's all I'll do."

"No!"

"You know you want it." Beau pulled up her shirt. She tried to stop him, but couldn't. He yanked it over her head, then stuck his face in her chest. "You smell so good." As he washed her chest with his spit, he reached behind her, undid her bra, and yanked it off.

Her breasts were divine. I almost forgot I was there to rescue her, they were so beautiful. But her clumsy attempts to get him off reminded me why I waited. Beau stood then and pulled off his own shirt and unzipped his jeans. She scrambled out of the bed and rolled onto the floor. I wanted to run in there, but he got up from the bed and grabbed her, pulling her off the floor. "Playing hard to get, huh, you really know how to turn a guy on." He intended to toss her on the bed but only succeeded in shoving her toward his nightstand.

Before he could grab her again, she picked up his night light and slammed it onto his head. He fell onto the bed. Dazed but not knocked out. I took that opportunity to walk into the room, like a drunkard who lost his way. I fell onto the floor and picked up her shirt in the process of getting up. I whispered to her. "I'm here to help you get away. Follow my lead."

She was slow on the uptake but clearly needed her shirt back so walked towards me.

Beau grunted at me. "Who do you think you are? Get the hell out of my room."

With his attention on me, Vanessa grabbed her shirt out of my hands and ran into the hall. She crumpled to the floor, crying.

Beau tried to sit up but grabbed his head and fell back down again. Either the lamp made a bigger impact than I thought or the drugs finally kicked in. He passed out. I didn't care.

I closed his door as I left the room, then knelt in front of her. "C'mon, let's get you cleaned up." I helped her up and to the bathroom. I put the toilet seat down and coaxed her to sit. I helped her put on her shirt, then ran a cold washcloth over her face and arms. It seemed to wake her a little. Then

I helped her up, escorted her out of the house, and drove her home. She was asleep by the time we got to her house. When I pulled into the driveway, I wasn't sure what to do. The house was dark. I had to help her inside somehow. I searched her pockets and found a set of keys. It took all my strength to pull her dead weight out of the car, but my mishandling woke her up a bit and I was able to half drag, half walk her to the front door. It took three tries to find the right key, but I opened the door. The nightlights provided enough light for me to see the living room on the right, so I dragged her over and let her fall onto the couch. I pulled off her shoes and put her keys on the coffee table, then left, locking the door behind me, thankful that nobody else woke up.

Beau's parents returned the next morning. They knew about the party so weren't too concerned, but when they walked into his room and tried to wake him, they couldn't. They called an ambulance, and he was rushed to the hospital, where, after viewing his blue-gray lips and finger tips, they administered Naloxone and started fluids.

Sadly, in my opinion, he recovered. The parents made a huge donation to the hospital and not a word of it made the papers. No matter, Vanessa ended their relationship, which opened the door for me. Or so I thought.

Valentine's Day approached. Vanessa and I now spoke to each other in class. Nothing major, but we said hello. Progress comes in all forms, I thought. She saw me differently now, especially since I got contacts and cut my hair in the latest style. She smiled at me. Perhaps she even saw me as her hero. Until she met him.

Craig Hunter, the eleventh-grade sexy saxophone player. To help the school band raise money, people hired him to perform the sexy saxophone routine. He crashed classes, lunches, and even went to people's houses after school. That day, when he came into our English class, he asked for her by name and played to her, around her, above her, and sat on the floor below her. He wore a pair of tight shorts and a fedora. All the girls in the class drooled over his muscled torso. I hoped to look that good in a few months, but I was a long way off with my workouts.

Before he left the room, he asked her to the Valentine's dance, and she agreed.

Shit, I should have asked sooner. Now I had to do something to stop it. I had two days before the night of the dance.

After school that day, I followed him. He walked to a gym about two blocks away. In the parking lot outside the gym he opened a car and threw his books into it. Then he pulled out a gym bag and walked into the gym. I followed him into the building.

Seeing all the people working on different machines proved a strange experience. People of all sizes and shapes worked out with no embarrassment. I didn't think I could do that.

"Can I help you?"

I jumped. How had I not have noticed the blonde at the counter. "Um, sure. How much does it cost to use this place?"

"That depends upon what you want to do. We have several membership tiers." She handed me a brochure. I took it and pretended to look at it while I scanned the room for Craig. I was about to hand the flyer back when I saw Craig come out of the locker room. He had the same gym bag but wore shorts and a tank top. He went to the free weights, reached into a side pocket of his bag, and pulled out a water bottle, which he placed on the bench.

"Hey."

"I turned to the girl.

"Do you want to sign up for any of them?"

"I'll think about it. Thanks." I turned and walked out the door. I knew exactly what to do.

The day of the dance, I skipped my morning classes and headed to the gym to see if his car was parked there. When I saw it, I knew that the gods were with me. If it weren't to be, the car would not have been there, right? It took a while to get the car open, between people coming and going out of the gym, and my three failed attempts. But eventually, it opened. I saw that he had two sealed bottles of water besides his metal drink bottle. For a minute, I thought my plan wasn't going to work. Would he drink bottled water if it was opened? But his metal bottle was full. I added the laxative to the full bottle. Then took a chance by opening one of the bottled waters and adding more to that. Maybe he wouldn't notice.

Waiting at the dance felt like hours but was only twenty minutes. Vanessa walked in with a bunch of other girls. They paused and looked around the room. I bit my lip to keep myself from running straight for her. Instead, I grabbed some sodas and sauntered over to the group. "Hi. Anyone need a drink?"

I could tell some of the girls hadn't shaken the "I don't talk to nerds" mentality, but Vanessa smiled and held out her hand. "I'll have a Coke, please."

My fingers brushed hers when I handed it to her. "Where's that saxophone guy?"

"Craig is home. He's come down with some stomach virus or something."

Laughter bubbled in my throat, but I tried to sound worried. "I hope you don't come down with it."

"Nah, I don't think so. We don't really hang out much."

Hope sprung in my heart, but then one of the other girls intruded by hanging onto Vanessa's shoulders. "C'mon, Ness, let's dance." Vanessa shrugged toward me and smiled, then left with the other girls.

Vanessa danced like a star. I thanked the heavens that I didn't have the courage yet to ask her to dance. There was no way I would embarrass myself on that floor in front of her. I added dance lessons to my list of things to learn.

After the dance, the days grew longer, my body grew muscles, and I found that I wasn't a bad dancer. Thank God for lunch money that paid for it all.

The last dance of the year, the senior dance, happened just before graduation. Every day I spent as much time with Vanessa, or rather near her, that I could. I still could not penetrate her circle of girlfriends, but at least she wasn't dating any more guys.

My chance to ask her happened in the library. By chance, we were doing research at the same time. We talked and then the question just popped out of my mouth. "Will you go to the dance with me?"

She looked surprised, then smiled. "I'd be happy to."

I refrained from doing what my brain told my body to do, which was jump up and scream, "She said yes!" I calmly told her I'd pick her up thirty minutes before so we could get pictures done. She agreed.

The day of the dance took forever to arrive, but when it did, I was ready. After getting a new haircut, and a manicure, I took a long, hot shower. I even shaved the small bits of fuzzy mustache off my face.

My nerves as I stood in the doorsill added to the sweat generated by the evening heat. Thank God my antiperspirant was working. When she opened the door, my jaw dropped. Gorgeous was too soft a word for how stunning she looked. I gave her the flowers. Her mom and dad took the obligatory pictures and promised to send me some.

I escorted her to the limo I had rented. The driver, as promised, took us on a loop around town before taking us to the Country Club.

We danced often and smiles lit up both our faces. But at one point, when I walked over to the bar to get sodas, Craig sauntered up to her and they spoke for several minutes. After that, she didn't smile so much and her gaze kept moving to where Craig danced with another girl.

The evening's end didn't go as I had wanted. By the time the last few songs were played, Vanessa expressed her fatigue and that she wanted to go home. I had parked my mom's car in the parking lot earlier that day so that I'd have a ride and I used it to drive her home.

I walked her to her front door. In my dreams, we stood there, arm in arm, and kissed for the first time. The reality was that she gave me a lame hug, said thanks, and walked into her house. That's when I knew that something was up.

I pulled out of her driveway and made my way to the park, then climbed to the roof of the bathrooms to watch her house. Within ten minutes, a car with several people and loud music pulled into her driveway. Vanessa ran out of the house and I watched Craig get out, open the passenger door, and help her into the car.

The betrayal hit me hard, almost knocking me backward. My heart and my head pounded out a race that nobody would win. I could not allow this to ever happen again. Vanessa was mine and I wasn't going to let anyone else have her.

After I calmed down a bit, I realized that I could talk to her. Yes, that's what I needed to do. I never told her how I felt and maybe if I did, she would reciprocate.

I knew her parents weren't home because they were heading out of town right before the dance started. I scouted around the house, thinking of ways to break into it, but found the back door unlocked. I would wait for her and when she returned, I'd tell her how I felt.

The sound of laughter and thumping noises woke me. Before I had time to register where I was, Vanessa's bedroom door opened and Craig pulled her inside. He started groping her and Vanessa looked like she was trying to fight him off.

How dare he! I grabbed the first thing I found. It was a twelve-inch cheerleading trophy with a solid base. I whacked Craig on the head and he instantly fell to the floor. Blood dripped from the white marble.

Vanessa's red eyes didn't quite register what was happening, as if she were drugged. But she recognized me and asked, "What're you doin' here?" She then stepped over Craig and flopped onto her bed trying hard to keep herself sitting upright.

I knelt down in front of her. "Vanessa, I love you. I want to spend the rest of my life with you!"

But she didn't hear me. Her eyes were glued to the blood staining her white rug. Her head started shaking back and forth. "No. What did you do?"

"Don't worry about him. I've taken care of him. It's you and me now, Vanessa. You and me forever."

Vanessa tried to stand, but I grabbed her hands and pulled her back down.

"Listen to me. These other guys are no good for you. They only want your body. But I love you."

Her voice rose higher. "No, what are you saying!" She slid to the floor and tried to help Craig, but I pulled her arm around to face me. I gripped both her arms. "Vanessa! Listen. You are mine. We are meant to be together, forever."

She wriggled loose and tried to get up. I couldn't let her walk out on me again. I tried to catch her and my hand landed on the trophy.

My other hand held her wrist and that's when she slapped me.

I don't know if it was survival instincts or just pure rage that she would hurt me, but my other hand closed over the trophy and I, controlled by my anger, hit her.

Blood spurted from the side of her head and she fell backward. I scooted around to help her sit up, but realized that she wasn't trying to move.

She just lay there, eyes open. Tears dripped from her red, swollen eyes.

"Oh Vanessa, I'm so sorry. I didn't mean to do that."

Her eyes fluttered, then closed. Her body fell limp. I couldn't feel her heart beat.

I rocked her and told her about my dreams and about how beautiful our lives, together, would have been.

I picked her up and placed her on the bed. Blood slowly oozed, but wasn't spurting everywhere. I got a wash cloth and tenderly cleaned up the blood from around her face. "Vanessa, my love. I'm so sorry. I'm sorry you didn't get a chance to see how much we meant to each other. We would have been great!"

Her cheeks, cleaned of the blood, still looked rosy. I ran my finger down them. "Worry no more, my love."

Salt in my mouth. Tears on my cheeks. I hadn't realized I was crying. I smoothed her hair behind her ears, folded her hands together on her chest, then tried to take a picture of her with my phone. My hands shook so bad, I couldn't keep the phone straight.

But that was okay, I had tons of pictures from the dance and didn't need another one, so I put it back into my pocket. I stared at her.

"I have to go now, Vanessa. You'll be okay. You won't ever again have to worry about stupid guys like him." I pointed at the still body of Craig on the floor.

Looking at Craig made me think of something. I picked up the statue, rubbed the place where I had touched it, then placed it in Craig's hand on the floor making sure to imprint his fingerprints all over it.

Then I bent over Vanessa one more time and kissed her lips.

"I love you."

We've all had them

You know you have

A passion for someone, or something, just out of reach

Finding Bubba

A Father's Love

*B*ridgette tiptoed down the stairs.

Callum looked up at her and whispered, "Is Scotty still crying?"

"He's not losing buckets anymore but he's not happy either. He wasn't quite asleep when I left but he's sucking his thumb. Are you sure you can't go look for it tonight?"

"Well, it's too late to go out tonight. I told him not to bring that darned toy on the tractor, but he must have stuffed it in his coat pocket."

"Callum," Bridgette slipped her hands around his waist. "Should we go with you in the morning?"

"No, there is a storm that's supposed to come through. The weatherman says it will be a light dusting, but it might be too cold for Scotty. I'll go out after I feed the animals. It's Saturday and you have no need to go anywhere."

"I knew there was a reason I married you, Callum McClusky."

The morning dawned cold and clear, but he smelled snow in the air. He fed the livestock, taking a moment to give their pregnant mare, Mrs. Crum, a little more attention and grain. "Hey girl, I'd take you out with me to find Bubba, but I don't want you getting too cold. Let's hope it stays clear, right?"

Callum started the tractor and drove the one and a half miles to the pumpkin fields, then shut it down to walk the pumpkin patch on foot. Yesterday, he and Scotty picked out the best pie pumpkins on the north side of the field, so that's where he started.

As he walked in the rows between long lines of pumpkins, snowflakes appeared. He pulled his hat further onto his head and zipped his fur-lined coat all the way up to his chin. The wind whipped up around his face and he wished he'd brought his scarf. Tucking his face into his parka, he continued looking for Bubba.

The air quickly became a snow-globe. Just as he turned to go back home, he noticed something moving. He ran over and looked down at the worn rabbit. Its lone ear flapped in the cold breeze. Bubba's one eye stared back at him.

"I know a little boy that's going to be happy you've decided to stop hiding."

Callum tucked Bubba firmly into the pocket of his parka. The tractor sat about a hundred yards away, but he could barely see it now with the curtain of snow in the air.

He hurried to the tractor and climbed into the seat. It wouldn't start. He debated hunkering down under it to wait out the storm but thought it better to make the trek home.

After walking three-tenths of a mile, Callum knew he'd made a mistake. The little storm grew into a winter hurricane. He couldn't see which direction to go. He knew the temperature must've dropped thirty degrees, because his snot froze before it reached his upper lip. His fingers felt icy pricks and the snow gathered around his footsteps. He thought of the sunny days driving past vineyards and orchards and wondered why the ever left SoCal.

He took some comfort in knowing a straight line connected the tractor to his front door. He continued in the same direction that he started. He didn't worry too much if he veered east. Then he'd run into the silo and he'd know how to proceed from there. But, if he veered west? Well, he didn't want to think about the vast open prairie.

Every few steps, he lifted his head. Snow took the opportunity to dive onto his neck. The icy cold flakes clung to his cold skin, but, seeing nothing, he tucked his chin and walked on.

After what felt like five miles, his lips quivered in the cold. If he didn't find the house soon, he might not make it. Pictures of Bridgette finding him encased in ice, like a Woolly Mammoth, filled his brain and fueled his feet.

Step, step, look. "Nothing."

Step, step, look. "What's that?"

The wind blew the leafless branches of the apple trees. As the tops swayed, snow danced.

Callum swallowed. He wondered if the trees waved or laughed at him. "See, aren't you glad you put us here now?"

Those darn apple trees! Bridgette convinced him, against his better judgment, to use their vacation money to purchase them. She wanted ten on each side of the drive to the front of the house. "It will be pretty and I can make you pie." He remembered her pleading eyes, those green eyes he couldn't ever resist. Then she added, "And it will remind us of home."

Though her pies always turned out good, the trees still bothered him. They made such a mess every August with apples rotting on the ground. Recently, he thought about pulling a few out and replacing them with trees that didn't make such a mess.

But now…he thanked heaven that they were there and even admitted that his attitude may have been a little petty. Perhaps he'd spend more time tending them instead of letting them go and then they could sell apples with the pumpkins.

His lips cracked as he smiled. "Bridgette, you are my hero."

The air thick with snow and the ground filling quickly made it difficult to walk, but he followed the trees to the front door. He threw it open and laughed like Santa. "Ho, ho, ho. Now I know how Santa feels."

Scotty ran up to him. "Bubba, did you find Bubba?"

Callum pulled off his frozen gloves, reached into his coat pocket, and pulled him out. "Here you go, Scotty."

Scotty hugged Bubba and then ran off asking the rabbit questions. "Did you like the snow? Did you see any Mooses?"

Bridgette walked over and helped Callum pull off his frozen parka. Then she kissed his red nose. "Thank you, Santa."

In all relationships there is give and take

Sometimes the capitulations

Turn out to be blessings

Broken, but Family

Love Between Siblings

I retreat into my head knowing that if I want to knock him over, I could. That if I want to make a scene where he wears my lunch on his shirt, I could. That if I want to kill him, I could.

Ignoring the taunts and the physical jabs makes me a better man. Well, as much a man as I can be in the twelfth grade. I have six more months to tolerate Chas and the shit he throws at me, and then I'm out of here for good.

Being labeled a nerd and a wuss since fifth grade gives me the honor of staying who I am. I am a nerd. But they don't know that I've been working out, learning Karate, and running every day. I wear baggy clothes so they don't see my muscles. I bought fake glasses two years ago for a play and loved how I could hide behind them. But I don't need them.

I put myself in harm's way to save other kids, knowing that if I couldn't stand it anymore, I could do something about it.

Chas goes after Nanette, my little sister who is a year behind me in school. I say little sister because she is smaller than me, but in terms of attitude and independence, she's much bigger. Besides being the cherished one in our home who can do no wrong, she's a stuck-up snob. I stay out of her way as much as I can. It's easy because she doesn't want to be found with a nerd close by. This doesn't bother me. I'm used to my sucky broken family. I can deal with it for a little longer.

Chas, though, isn't teasing her, he pants for her. He struts around her like a peacock because Nanette is gorgeous. Think Barbie meets Audrey Hepburn. Until recently, she kept him at arm's length, but that changed when he showed up at school with a new Corvette convertible.

I'm not sure he even knows I'm her brother. But his attentions to me get worse and, judging by what I overhear during Nanette's phone conversations, which she never tries to hide, she's keeping him out of her pants on purpose.

As her older brother, I feel duty-bound to let her know that this could seriously backfire, but she doesn't care and flips me off. I shrug my shoulders and walk on. I did my bit.

We rarely interact for the next few months and now it's almost prom night. Nanette and Chas are on the slate for King and Queen. I don't know how she's done it, but I don't think they've had intercourse yet. I've seen some heavy petting sessions, but Nanette is controlled. She can also kill a fly with a look.

Father and Mother are tickled that she's where she is and with the richest kid on the block. My mother obtained a degree in physics but acts like a Stepford wife, and is a driving force behind Nanette's success as a beautiful "catch." Father doesn't mind either because Chas's father golfs with him.

I'm not a total loser in my parents' eyes. I got a scholarship to MIT and they are pleased. I haven't told them, and won't tell them until it's too late, that I don't plan to go there. I have other plans that will take me far away from this supercilious life.

Prom night arrives. Mother and Father have left already on a cruise leaving Nanette to fend for herself. Nobody cares if I go to prom or not, and I'm not. A gaggle of giggling girls is downstairs drinking mimosas, doing their hair, and who knows what else they are doing. It's their lives, not mine.

But at some point, before they leave, I feel a responsibility well up in me to at least give them a parental warning.

I hear the beeping of cars announcing the arrival of the peacocks and the girls line up at the door doing last-minute touches to their hair. I mosey to the middle of the staircase and lean over.

I tell them all to have a fun evening and if they have any problems to call me. I'll be home manning the phones. Nanette lifts her middle finger and tells me to go fuck myself. The laughing increases until they are out the door. They leave it hanging open, so I move farther down the steps to close it.

I look around the house at the mess they made and don't care. I order pizza, watch TV until it arrives, and then head back up to my room to work on the video game I'm designing.

I barely hear my phone ring through the fog of my dream, but I manage to find it.

Nanette is breathing heavily and I hear loud, muffled music. She tells me she's scared, locked in a bathroom, and doesn't know what to do. I hear banging and voices and Nanette cries. "Sean, They're going to break the door down. Help."

"Where are you?"

"I'm at Chas's house."

"I'm coming."

I'm don't waste much time getting dressed, just throwing on the first T-shirt I find and baggy shorts. I don't think twice about driving Mom's Audi, and I arrive at Chas's house quicker than the map's GPS says I will.

The house is a mansion. Kids are flowing out the front door and around the lawn like ants. How the hell will I find her?

I park at the front door and someone tells me that parking is out back. I ignore them. What are they going to do, call the cops? I doubt it.

Since I have no idea where she might be, I start asking about the location of the bathrooms. I check all on the first floor, then fly up the large curved staircase to the second floor.

A scream sounds from down the hall and I run toward the room. Chas's two friends hold Nanette on a bed, her ass is in the air, while Chas's dick is drunkenly trying to find a home.

I don't hesitate. My foot flies right into his testicles with a roundhouse kick and he flies onto the floor, screaming curses at me.

His two friends look at me and only see the shy nerd they've always seen. I tell them to let her go. They refuse and flip her onto her back, one of them climbing on top of her, grabbing her dress and ripping it. The other stands and approaches me.

He has at least five inches and twenty pounds on me, but he's drunk and one swipe of my leg knocks him onto his ass.

I dive toward the man on top of Nanette and, grabbing his shoulders, let the momentum carry me and him off the bed. We land with a thud on the floor with him on top of me. I see the smile in his eyes, the delight that he has me where he wants me, before he pulls back his fist.

His mistake. The light in his eyes leads my thumbs right to the sockets and I push them in. He screams in agony, grabs at his eyes, and rolls away.

The second guy is waiting for me at the door. I pull off my T-shirt and hand it to Nanette. "Cover up and get behind me."

I see the surprise in her eyes as she notices my biceps, but she listens.

The guy in the doorway smirks as if he knows something that I don't. In my periphery, I see Chas. I pull out my pocket knife, tossing it accurately into his thigh. He drops the lamp he carried, I guess to hit me with, and screams in pain, again.

I turn to the guy at the door, who puts his hands up in surrender, then runs from the room.

I grab Nanette's hands and gently guide her out of the room, out of the house, and into the car.

I slowly drive home, allowing her time to think. It allows me to think too. How will all this change my life? I don't want to change anything. I want to be invisible until I leave.

I glance at her when she starts softly sobbing. "Are you okay?"

She nods but continues to cry.

The tears bring memories smashing into my brain. Like putting bandages on her knees, chasing bugs off her chair, and teaching her to ride a bike because Mother and Father were too busy.

I pull into the driveway and open her door for her. She just sits there, sobbing, so I take her hand and pull her into the house. I nudge her to her room and help her lie down on her bed. I get a hot washcloth to wipe the mascara off her cheeks. It doesn't work well, but at least most of it is gone.

This pulls her out of her stupor long enough to smile at me and call me a hero.

I wake the next morning, trepidation nipping at my brain. But I didn't need to worry. When I walk into the kitchen, she's standing at the coffee machine. She turns to look at me. "I fucked up. But that doesn't change jack shit."

I nod. "Okay."

But it does change things. She breaks up with Chas and, even with my mother and father's urging, she remains boyfriend-free to this day.

She still ignores me and treats me like scum, but the parents make her go to my graduation. I walk across the stage with several honors that embarrass me, and I see my mother and father acting like they did all the work. I can't wait to surprise them with my future goals.

My plan is to take my new Mazda and drive away. Yes, I let them buy me a car, I ain't stupid. They think I'm going to summer orientation in Massachusetts, but I'm driving to Florida to live on the beach and work on a bachelor's in game design. They won't know any of that until I'm gone and they read the note I mailed to them yesterday.

Nanette comes up to me and asks me if I want to get a coffee before I drive away. I'm stumped by this, but she doesn't wait for an answer. Instead, she gets into her BMW and pulls out of the driveway.

I wave to Mother and Father like I'm the president sitting in a car during a parade, then hop in the Mazda and follow her.

She doesn't drive to a coffee shop, but instead drives to the beach where we used to build sandcastles together. She sits on the hood of the car and motions for me to join her there.

We sit quietly, watching the waves in the distance.

"Thank you."

The words surprise me. "For what?"

"For not making an issue of, you know, what happened on prom night. I don't think I would have survived had you made it an issue, or if Mother and Father found out."

"You're my little sister. I know we're not close, but I watched you grow up. I mean, I hope you come out of this stuck-up bitch phase soon, but I'm here for you."

She drops her chin and says quietly, "Yes, you are. Thank you."

I laugh. "You won't thank me in a few days when Mother and Father get my letter and you are the only one to hear them rant."

She looks at me with the question in her eyes and I tell her my plans.

The smile that grows on her face gives me hope that she might one day be a decent person.

We watch the waves a bit longer and she gets up. "Don't be a stranger, you know my number."

"Will do."

I get behind my wheel and send her a salute from the window. She ignores me, pulls out of the parking space, and drives away. I guess some things take more time.

Some families are broken

But, when attacked

They become a fortress together

We're All Expendable, Get Over It

Self-Love

*H*ow long will the pain last? Will I die before I feel it? Will the world miss me?

My internal trilogy brought me to the brink several times in my life. Once, I held a pocket knife (that would have hurt like hell) to my wrist only to be drawn away by the banging of the dorm room door as my neighbor from down the hall came barging in. She was already halfway drunk, so she didn't notice.

"Hey Ally, you want to go get something to drink?"

I am quite sure my life would be different had the drinking age in West Virginia not been eighteen at the time. But it was, and my early adult years were mired in a thick veil of alcohol.

Paired with this new way of drowning out the world, I found that college boys had no problem screwing an ugly girl. I don't see myself now as ugly, but back then, I had just finished ten years of my peers telling me I was a dog. I soon equated sex with beauty and acceptance. As long as I gave it, I was loved. My invincible self did just about anything.

Like the time I went skinny dipping with total strangers. I was playing pool with some folks that weren't from around town and they bet that if I didn't win, I'd go with them. I must have lost, because the memory of stripping and jumping in the cold water of Cheat Lake at 2 a.m. still makes me smile. But I can't remember how I got there or got home after.

Once, I invited myself to go rappelling with a group of rock climbers. Teasingly, they told me to meet them at the top of the mountain the next day. By the looks on their faces when I arrived, I could tell they hadn't expected me. The one guy smiled and said, "Okay then, here's what to do."

I went down just fine. The fifty feet of exhilaration boosted my ego. The guy that came after me fainted and fell. He hit the rocks and bounced. He was alive but not conscious. There was no blood or visible broken bones. We didn't touch him; we were afraid we might damage him in some way. He started groaning just before the EMTs arrived. They put an IV in him and missed his vein, hitting an artery instead. Blood spattered everywhere. When they put him in the ambulance, he was woozy but talking and laughing. I never saw any of them again.

Sometimes I'd wake up in places I'd never been before, totally dependent upon the other people around me. It was times like these, my body exhausted from the drinking and self-deception, that a self-loathing anguish filled my entire being. That's when the trilogy hit the hardest. How long will the pain last? Will I die before I feel it? Will the world miss me?

In my senior year of high school, I joined the Army Reserves with my two sisters. It was my first attempt at living life for me, not for others. Much to my surprise, and contrary to the "Be All That You Can Be" banners, the military wasn't about me. I still had to follow others' directions, follow others' rules, and do my best to please my drill sergeant, then my warrant officer.

About three years into being a member of the 354th Ordnance Co of Morgantown, West Virginia, where, after a summer training to become an office clerk, they reassigned me to drive forklifts, I transferred to the 249th Army Band in Fairmont, West Virginia. That little band, full of retired band directors and high school band geeks that never had musical training, was not the real Army. What happened during that time cannot be believed, yet the drinking, the stupid games, and the coddling of us female soldiers, happened. It was just what my fragile ego needed to tank faster than ever.

What kept me from jumping off the bridge? How did I ride through college traversing valleys so low? Why did I not walk through death's open invitation?

Need.

Not mine, but others'.

Somehow, my willingness to live became directly related to how much I was needed. It didn't matter what I was needed for, just that I felt I was necessary.

I am a musical person, but I don't need music. However, my mother needed me to be good at it. I was her promising child. I couldn't fail.

My piano teacher needed me to win competitions. My college professors needed me to shine better than the rest.

My students needed me to teach.

Did I like being a piano teacher? It had its ups and downs, but I didn't do it because of a passion for music. I did it because others needed me to. My family also needed the extra cash.

There are few things in life that I did not do for others, but for me. Having a family was all for me.

I remember when, after wallowing low in the valley and staring at the door to death, I reached out to the invisible one, the God that I was brought up to believe in. The God who lived in the church down the street and never came to our house. The God of the people, a social gathering of like minded individuals. I prayed. Something I've done very little of. "Dear God, I just want a family and someone to love. Is it that hard to find?"

Seven years later, as I started my master's at Temple, I found him. I found a man who loved me with all my warts, including the inner ones. The ones that don't show on the outside.

Yet, even after marrying him and having two wonderful children, I found my mind wandering; wondering. The valley seems inviting when you feel like nobody hears you.

Fast forward through having my first baby while my husband fought in Operation Desert Storm, a couple of dogs, cats, a horse, trauma, dozens of gymnastic meets, selling cookies, numerous weekends carting my teen son to bike races that were hours away, camping in the rain to save money, high school and college graduations, two weddings, and a grandbaby.

Now I'm sixty-one. What the hell? I can't define myself by my friends anymore. I can't define myself through my kids. My husband is self-sufficient. The house is paid for. Nobody needs me.

If I were to die right now, people would miss me, but they don't need me to continue in their own lives. Life would go on. Nothing would suddenly stop because I wasn't there anymore. I'm expendable.

And somehow, knowing that I'm expendable has given me freedom.

Do I love me? Not always. I'm lazy, stubborn, and can be quite domineering. (Probably from having to do for others for so long.)

Do I still gravitate to activities where someone needs me? Yes, I do. Don't fault me for being the on-call babysitter. It's part of my "I'm doing what I want to" plan.

Sometimes, I still see the valley. I've walked in it so many times, I actually feel comfort when I go there. But the door never appears.

I am expendable. Nobody needs me.

I'm over it.

Now I can figure out what I want to be when I grow up. I think I want to be an author.

I you haven't teetered on the edge of self-loathing

You're lucky

The Dog Pile

Love in Forgiveness

When the car pulled into the driveway, I felt my muscles tighten and that familiar flurry of, not butterflies, but something more malevolent, stirring in my chest. Why were they here? They knew how I felt?

Nasty words from the past rushed to my brain, but I was an adult now. I could handle this. I took a deep breath and waited for their knock.

Normally, Bella, my beautiful boxer, would stand guard next to me. She was always a good judge of character and chased off many salesmen and bill collectors, but when I opened my door to my sisters, she wagged her tail, bonking my knee while she did it, and begged for pets and hugs. "Traitor," I thought.

Margie, Susan, and Brenda, in that order, were all about two years apart in age. I was four years younger than Brenda. I hadn't seen them for over three years since our mom's funeral.

I let them in. I wondered at their pieces of luggage. Where did they think they were staying? From behind them came a man holding leashes attached to three dogs. He also came through the door.

Bella immediately set about saying hello and when the man asked, "Are we okay with them in here?" I couldn't say no. Bella made the rules in this house.

After I nodded, he released the dogs from their leashes and the four of them ran through the doggie door to the backyard with yelps of wonder and joy.

The man, it turned out, was Maggie's new husband, Dan. (A wedding I did not attend.) He shook my hand and promptly followed the dogs out the back door.

My sisters, leaving their luggage by the door, plowed their way into my living room. A place they knew well since we all grew up in this house. While I, the youngest, stayed to care for my ill mom, they went on their merry life doing whatever.

After expressing my ingrained sense of hostess-ness, offering coffee and cake, I got straight to the point. "Why are you here?"

Before they could answer, Dan and all the dogs returned from the backyard. Dan helped himself to coffee and the dogs all piled into Bella's bed. I couldn't believe they all squeezed in and, within minutes, were a pile of smelly, contented, snoring dogs.

My gaze wandered to the bags by the door. Then it landed on my sisters and I realized Bella had done it again. "Would you all like to spend the night here? It's getting late and I'm not sure the Motel 6 down the road is up to your standards." I had an image of the four of us all snoring on my bed. I shook my head. I wouldn't go that far, but the house had plenty of empty rooms.

Maggie stole a glance at Susan and Brenda, then blurted out, "We're sorry."

Speechless, all I could do was swallow the words that I intended to say.

Susan continued. "Lauren, we are sorry for so many things; we can't count them."

Brenda started crying quietly but muttered, "And we are sorry for being such horrible older sisters."

It was at this time that Bella wiggled her way out from under the pile of dogs and came over to Brenda. She put her chin on Brenda's knee and looked at her with eyes that only a dog can make. Eyes that said, "I love you, no matter what."

I'm not sure how I would have responded to any of this without Bella showing me the way. I stood up, walked over to Brenda, and hugged her. "I'm sorry too. For everything."

I looked at Maggie and Susan and they came over to join the hug. Then the three other dogs came over and we were one big pile on my couch.

Dan, however, took another approach. "Who's hungry? I'll order the pizza."

About the Author

Ally is an alter ego. She's the woman who writes from over 40 years of adulting on this earth. She's the Yin of the whole that writes about all the things her other half won't. She writes about love, friendship, and heartache. Her stories range from happily ever after endings to horrific, macabre endings that lead to loss and death. Many of her stories aren't meant for the faint of heart.

Love, There's All Kinds is Ally's debut novel. But there are more on the way!

https://allyallowinter.blogspot.com/
https://www.facebook.com/AllyAauthor/
https://www.instagram.com/ally_a_writes/

Don't be afraid to love.

Unless it's the wrong kind…

If you liked this collection of stories,

please consider adding a review on Amazon.